Stetson's Storm

Kathleen Ball

DEDICATION

I dedicate *Stetson's Storm* to all of my wonderful cousins, both in the United States and in Ireland. You have all been amazingly supportive and someday I hope to go to Ireland to meet a lot of you.

Thank you to Stetson, my brother Mike's dog for lending me his name.

And as always, I dedicate my novel to my three guys, Bruce, Steven, and Colt because I love them.

CHAPTER ONE

The bells above the diner door rang eerily in the still of the night. Storm startled then whirled around. It'd been quiet all night; the graveyard shift usually was. The money wasn't the greatest, but somehow she managed. Her eyes widened and her heart raced faster. It couldn't be, but it was. Stetson had returned.

He noticed her but Storm saw no sign of recognition in his eyes. Maybe it was a good thing. She knew she looked drawn and tired. The circles under her eyes never seemed to disappear anymore, her hair no longer shone, and she was rail thin.

His lack of recognition cut deep and the pain in her heart overwhelmed her. He didn't remember her, but she hadn't forgotten him for one day during his five-year absence.

Grabbing the glass coffee pot, she quickly walked over to where he sat at the counter. "Coffee?"

"Sure, honey," Stetson replied, looking over his shoulder at a group of new customers.

Disappointment filled her being as she poured the hot liquid into his mug. "Anything else?"

"Uh, no."

Storm nodded, put the pot down, and walked into the kitchen to regroup. He unnerved her.

"She's not the one for you." Storm heard one customer comment.

"I'm not interested," Stetson's familiar voice responded.

"Good thing. She's got a bit of a reputation." The busybody female's voice sounded sultry, as though she wanted Stetson for herself.

Tears welled up in Storm's eyes waiting for his reply. All she heard was the ringing of the bells. She hoped she hadn't been stiffed again. Last time it had come out of her pocket. She walked back behind the counter. Stetson had left. He was always leaving.

Storm had finally and firmly written him off, but her heart didn't agree. Thankfully, she had a strong mind. No man would ever play her for a fool again. Stetson had cost her everything, her home, her family. Most of the members of the town wouldn't talk to her.

If it hadn't been for Nellie, Stetson's sister, she wouldn't have survived the last five years.

She had to admit he looked damn good in his jeans, boots, and blue chambray shirt. Blue always brought out his striking, sky blue eyes. He had a few more lines on his face, his handsome, tanned, chiseled face. His thick blond hair curled out of control, and she had to stop herself from remembering how it felt to run her fingers through it.

He'd filled out. He had a man's body now, with big shoulders and a slender waist. He probably had his share of women over the last five years. The thought crushed her. She'd been left to suffer and he'd gone on to fame.

It still stung that Stetson never even said goodbye. He just up and left town one day while Storm had waited and waited to no avail. Finally, she had to tell her daddy she was pregnant.

Mentally shaking herself, Storm grabbed the coffee pot and refilled the customers' mugs. Things were different now. She was different. She had a fine son that looked like them both since they both were blue eyed with blond hair. Scotty reminded her of Stetson.

Her replacement was late again. *Damn Bailey anyway!* She knew that Storm had to get back home to her son, and each day she seemed to take delight in being late.

Lasso Springs had been a fine town when Storm was growing up. It was rustic and small. Everyone seemed to know each other. There had always been a row of shacks at the edge of town. Rundown places with running water, barely. That was her home now.

No one would hire her. She was no longer the right kind of person. Their archaic outlook filled her with fury. The community of Lasso Springs had turned their backs on her. The only job she could get was the graveyard shift at the diner. Making ends meet became almost impossible, but she did. She provided for Scotty and was proud she was a good mother.

Looking at the clock again, Storm sighed. She knew she couldn't complain. Bailey was a spiteful young woman with a waspish tongue and Storm always got the feeling Bailey would love to get her fired.

Storm heard laughter coming from the kitchen. Bailey finally showed up. It only took her another half hour to make her way to the front of the diner.

Storm didn't wait for an apology that would never come. The cash drawer had been counted by Frank. Free to go, she brushed by Bailey, gathered her things, and left. It was a good walk home, but Storm couldn't afford a car. The dark clouds overhead looked ominous. Sure enough, it began to pour. Storm looked up into the heavens and asked, "Why me?" She knew the answer. She'd trusted and loved the wrong person.

*****

Sighing in relief, Stetson Scott made the turn onto the dirt road leading to the ranch. He was tired. The coffee at the diner helped a bit, but driving sixteen hours had taken its toll. Rubbing the back of his neck, he could feel the knots of tension.

He had a lot to do before he'd be able to get any shuteye. He had to see to his horses in the trailer. They needed tending first. Then he'd deal with his sister.

The big iron sign that read "Scott Ranch" hung at an awkward angle across the drive. Stetson was concerned. Granted, his father was dead, but he always took pride in the ranch. Driving further, the evidence of neglect showed even more. The fences had holes in them. The barn looked to be in disrepair, and the house needed a coat of paint.

It seemed as though he'd been gone much longer than five years. Something was dreadfully wrong. The Scott ranch had always been one of the most prosperous in the county. Judging from its current condition, Stetson doubted that to be true anymore.

The sun was making itself known in the big Texas sky. No matter where he went he always missed Texas. Getting out of the truck, he took a deep breath of the sweet air.

The screen door flew open and Nellie came running out. She was a welcome sight. Her light brown hair trailed behind her as she ran to him. Nellie's smiles were always beaming. They could make a person feel as though the sun shined only for her.

Stetson opened his arms, grabbed her up, and swung her around. Her laughter was a balm to his heart.

"Looking good, Sis," he said, putting her down. "You're as pretty as a newborn filly."

"Always with the horse talk," she teased. "I'm glad you're home."

Home, Stetson hadn't called any place home in years. He wasn't sure he wanted to call this ranch home again. "I got your letter and lit out."

"I knew you'd come." Nellie's eyes filled with unshed tears.

"It's been bad?"

Nellie nodded and walked into his embrace. Stetson could feel her body rack with sobs. He wished he could feel something, anything about his father's passing. He just felt numb and it bothered him.

"Why didn't you get in touch with me sooner? This place looks run down."

"Papa wouldn't let me. He'd rather we starve than get help."

"I'm sorry, Nellie." Stetson rubbed his hands up and down her back.

Nellie pulled away and smiled at him. "You're here now, that's all that matters. The ranch is yours now, and I just know you can turn it around."

Stetson frowned. "What do you mean? I figured I was cut out of the old man's will."

"He left everything to you. I got nothing."

"Oh, Nellie, I'm sorry. Listen, I have to take care of Rosie and Bandit, and then I'll be in. Have some coffee ready for me?"

"Yes, I'll make it extra strong, just the way you like it."

"Thanks."

Stetson watched her walk away. What the hell happened around here? He hadn't planned to stay for long, but he couldn't leave Nellie with this mess. He'd get the ranch back into shape, sign it over to Nellie, and get the hell out.

Damn his father anyway. It was his way or the highway, and Stetson chose the highway. He loved horses and planned to be a rancher someday after his rodeo days were over. His father couldn't accept it.

He led Bandit into the barn, shocked to see so many empty stalls. Maybe if he had stayed. No, he couldn't think that way. His father left him no choice with his ultimatum: stop doing rodeo or leave. Stetson left and never looked back.

Leading Rosie into the barn, he remembered better times with the stalls all filled with champion horses and ranch hands aplenty. Maybe his father had been sick these last few years.

Stetson settled his horses and strode to the house. The screen door closed behind him with a loud bang. Some things were the same. The house appeared clean. Nellie had been doing a good job. Thankful the coffee was ready, he poured himself a cup.

"Still drink it black?" Nellie asked from the doorway that led into the family room.

"I'm still a cowboy aren't I?"

Nellie laughed. "I forgot a cowboy drinks his coffee black and eats his steak raw."

Stetson smiled. "We need to talk. What the hell went on around here? Where are the horses?"

Nellie put her hands in her jean pockets and stared at the floor. "It was my entire fault," she whispered.

"What does that mean?" Stamos asked, gently.

"I refused to marry the man Papa picked out for me." She glanced up to his blue eyes, pleading for understanding. "I wanted to marry for love. I would have left, but I had nowhere to go. I stayed and kept house, but Papa wouldn't talk to me, only to criticize. So, you see, it's all my fault."

"Is that why he left the ranch to me?"

"You are the lesser of two evils."

Stetson gave her a slight smile. "You could never be evil, honey. Who did he want you to marry?"

"Pat McCrory."

Stetson widened his eyes in surprise. "Storm's father?"

Nellie nodded and stared at the floor again.

"He wanted you to marry that old geezer? What was

6

he thinking?"

Nellie walked over to Stetson and put her hand on his arm. "He wanted to stop the revenge that Pat was extracting. The price for him to stop was me."

Stetson put his coffee down and hugged Nellie. "It's not your fault. What the hell had McCrory's tail in a knot?"

"You left Storm without saying goodbye and we didn't know how to reach you."

"What does that have to do with anything?"

"Stetson, she was pregnant with your son."

Stetson stiffened and let go of Nellie. "What?" he asked in a harsh whisper.

"McCrory figured you owed him, so he wanted me. He threw Storm out as soon as he found out. She works at the diner, graveyard shift."

Stetson closed his eyes. It couldn't be. The waitress couldn't have been his Storm. Surely, he would have known. She had his son. His heart raced as his whole world turned upside down.

*****

Exhausted, Storm made herself a pot of coffee. Finding time to sleep had been an ongoing problem. By the time she got home from the diner, Scotty was up and ready to start his day.

She couldn't afford to send him to preschool or any type of daycare. She'd been blessed that her next-door neighbor, Lottie Burns, watched him at night for free. Lottie had no family of her own, and it seemed she had adopted Storm and Scotty. Storm didn't know what she'd do without the older woman.

"I think I'm going to the park today, Mommy," Scotty said, smiling up at her with hopeful eyes, Stetson's eyes.

"We'll see." The other children weren't very kind to Scotty, and the mothers ignored her. Scotty didn't seem to notice, but Storm didn't like to expose him to their attitudes.

Scotty frowned and shook his head. "That means no," he said with a heavy sigh.

Storm bent down and picked him up. "Now why do you say that?"

"We'll see is always a no."

Storm smiled and ruffled his hair. "Well that hardly seems right. Let me get changed and then we'll go."

"All right!" Scotty cheered, jumping out of her arms.

They walked to the park, holding hands, much to Scotty's objection. He thought holding hands was for babies. The park was practically empty, and some of the burden on her shoulders lightened.

Scotty raced to the slide and Storm sat on a nearby bench. It was nearly spring, Storm's favorite time of the year. The whole world seemed fresh and new with endless possibilities. Not for her, she conceded. She tried to hold on to hope and determination, that maybe someday but life had worn her down and she had to finally admit dreams weren't reality.

Storm's heart lurched when she spotted the male striding across the grass. She'd been expecting him, but she hoped somehow he wouldn't find out about Scotty.

He looked so fine. Rodeo riding had made his arms bulge with strength. His eyes were the same bright blue as their son's. He wasn't smiling. In fact, he appeared down right angry. Storm felt intimidated, but she had to hold her ground.

There was no smile, no greeting. Stetson sat next to her on the bench and watched Scotty go up the ladder and slide down. "So it's true," he finally commented.

Storm didn't want to look at him. She didn't want him looking at her. She knew she looked like something the cat dragged in. She was no longer the bright-eyed teenager he knew. The last five years had taken a toll on her.

"He's mine," Stetson sighed.

"No, he's mine. No one else's, just mine," Storm

retorted, still not looking at him.

"Look, Storm--"

"Save it for someone that wants to hear it. I waited and waited; now it's too late."

Stetson ignored her as Scotty came running over full of energy.

"Mommy, I'm all dirty."

Storm laughed. "So what else is new, kiddo?"

Scotty stole a look at Stetson, and then he stared. "You look like me!"

Stetson chuckled. "You look like me too."

Scotty turned to his mother. "He must be handsome, Mommy, just like me, right?"

Storm shifted her gaze to Stetson. Their eyes locked. "Yes, Scotty, he is handsome. Scotty, this is Stetson Scott, an old friend."

"Howdy," Scotty said.

Storm watched as Stetson swallowed hard. She couldn't read the array of emotions that came across his face, but she could tell he was touched to meet his son.

"Hey, my name is Scotty and your last name is Scott. You can change it to be like mine if ya want. Then we can both be Scotty."

"You might be on to something, Scotty. It would be fun if we had the same name." He stared right at Storm with his right eyebrow raised.

Storm had had enough. Her nerves began to frazzle. "Well, nice to see you again. Maybe we'll see each other in another five to ten years."

Stetson gave her one of his knowing smiles that she hated. "Oh, I don't know, that might be too long to wait."

"Can you come and visit us?" Scotty asked, jumping up and down.

Stetson chuckled. "You can bet on it, Scotty."

Storm stood up and grabbed Scotty's hand, leading him away.

"Did you hear that, Mommy? He's going to visit!"

"Yes I heard," Storm said, feeling the weight of the world on her shoulders again.

CHAPTER TWO

"How the hell did Storm end up in that decrepit shack? Good God, she's raising my son there? It looks as though a good strong wind would cause it to collapse," Stetson asked his sister as soon as he returned from town.

Nellie winced. "You went by her place?"

"Yes, damn it!" he yelled, pounding his fist on the kitchen table. The dishes rattled.

"I'm sorry, Stetson." Nellie reached out to put her hand on top of his.

"Sorry doesn't cut it." Stetson immediately regretted yelling at Nellie as she cringed away. "I'm sorry. I don't mean to take it out on you."

"Papa wouldn't let me contact you. He was beyond mad when you left. He never expected that any of his wishes would be defied," Nellie explained with tears in her eyes. "I wasn't allowed to acknowledge Scotty. I did what I could for them. I left food and clothes on their front porch. I knew Storm wouldn't accept it if I rang the bell. She's got too much pride to accept help."

"You always were the kind one in the family."

Nellie looked at him with her deep blue eyes and shook her head. "I was the coward. I stayed."

"Nellie, don't think that way. So, the old bastard wouldn't acknowledge his grandson. No big surprise there."

Stetson took a good look at his sister. She'd grown up while he was gone. Her light brown hair looked healthy and shiny. She wore it in a long braid down her back. She still had the longest legs he'd ever seen.

Stetson got up and grabbed the coffee pot, refilling both mugs. "What about you? Any young beaus I should know about?"

Nellie turned bright red. "No one." She shook her head.

Stetson knew she was lying. "You can tell me, Nel."

Nellie stared at the floor then lifted her head and gazed at him. He could see the fear in her eyes. "It's me, Nel, you can trust me."

Nellie nodded. "Most of the ranch hands left when Papa began to have financial problems. Only Joe remained."

"Joe Sullivan?"

Nellie blushed. "Yes. He's a good man."

"Good choice."

"What are you going to do about Storm?"

"Do?"

"Well, you can't let her live in that shack. She's your responsibility, her and Scotty."

Stetson frowned. "I'll have to get full custody of my son."

Nellie shook her head and pointed her finger at him. "Over my dead body! Storm has been through hell and back trying to raise your son. You can't just take him away."

"I guess I haven't given it enough thought," he admitted.

"You need to go get them and bring them here to live."

Stetson felt a sudden fear in his heart. Unfortunately, he knew Nellie was right. He just didn't want any entanglements. A son he could handle, but things with Storm had been too intense. It had hurt too much to leave.

Stetson walked out to the unkempt barn. The red paint was peeling and the doors looked none too sturdy. A quick glance at the roof left him cringing. It was unlike his father to let anything go to ruin.

"Hey, Joe, long time no see."

Joe stopped shoveling the old hay in mid shovel. A big grin graced his face. "Thank God above! Someone else to muck out the stalls."

Stetson looked at his childhood friend. "No gray hairs in that black hair of yours yet?"

"I'm just as surprised you aren't balding," Joe shot back.

Stetson smiled. "You know my hair has always drawn all the women to me."

"That many, huh?"

Stetson stopped smiling. "No, a few dates, but no one special."

"Seen Storm yet?" Joe asked.

"You mean the mother of my child?"

"That would be the one." Joe's voice sounded serious.

"I can understand Nellie not calling me, but I would have expected you to let me know I had a son," Stetson said, shaking his head.

"I would have, but I was told you already knew and that's why you left. I've been mad at you for years."

"Who told you that? Never mind, I can guess. It was my father wasn't it?"

Joe nodded. "Said you denied it was yours and you took off."

Stetson hit the barn wall with his fist. "Damn him! I didn't know. My father didn't want me riding rodeo.

He insisted that I stop or leave. I left."

"Sorry, buddy, I should have known you wouldn't have walked away from your responsibilities."

"Can't go back." Stetson tried to calm down. "What the hell happened to the ranch?"

"We can jaw as we work. Lots to do around here," Joe replied.

"Okay, let's get the stalls cleaned and you can fill me in."

*****

Storm sat on the old couch, tilting her head back and closing her eyes. She finally got Scotty down for his nap. Usually she napped too, but she already knew she wouldn't be able to sleep.

All Scotty had done all morning was ask about Stetson. Question upon question, so many, too many questions. Her head was spinning and her heart was being ripped out of her chest, yet again.

It was no big surprise to see him at the park. She knew he'd want to see his son. He just didn't want to see her. She could tell. Storm had been preparing for that moment ever since Stetson's father died. However, no amount of preparing could shield the pain.

She longed to scream at him. She needed him to know what his decision to go the rodeo circuit had cost her. She wanted to tell him that he was a selfish, unfeeling coward. Sadly, part of her wanted to be in his strong arms. It would feel so good to gather strength from him, but it wouldn't happen.

It wasn't fair. She had finally gotten over him. The first year she waited and waited, fully believing Stetson would come back to her. After Scotty was born, she was convinced he'd be at the hospital with a bouquet of flowers for her. All she got was painful disappointments, one right after another.

Scotty, and how to support him, took most of her time and thoughts. Storm did think about Stetson every day. She couldn't look at Scotty without thinking about his father. They were so alike.

It had taken a while, but she had accepted her fate. As far as she was concerned, Stetson was just an intrusion.

Storm heard Scotty waking from his nap and smiled. No matter how hard life had been, she wouldn't trade Scotty for anything. Her dreams for herself no longer mattered, making sure Scotty had a chance to obtain his was important.

The pitter-patter of little feet warmed her. So far, Scotty was unaware of what people said about her. He'd be starting kindergarten next year, and the thought brought fear to Storm's heart.

She hadn't dated or gone out at night. She spent all her free time with Scotty, and she worked damn hard, but there were people in Lasso Springs who believed Stetson's father when he denied that Scotty was Stetson's. Her own father throwing her out of the house sealed her fate.

Scotty ran and leaped onto Storm. His slightly crooked smile reminded her of Stetson. One day, she'd be able to look at Scotty and not think of Stetson and his betrayal. Right now, she had to make sure that Stetson's return didn't hurt Scotty.

"Is that man coming back?" Scotty asked, his eyes filled with hope.

"I don't know, kiddo, maybe."

"You don't like Mr. Scott?"

"Mr. Scott is an old friend. Let's go to the store. I'll make spaghetti for dinner."

"All right!" Scotty cheered, hopping off her and racing for the door.

*****

Stetson scrutinized the immense Texas sky, longing he could wish on a star. Life would be so simple if wishes were granted. Inhaling the fragrant air, he smiled. He missed being here. He finally realized it was pure anger that kept him away. Guilt rocked him as he thought about the conversation he'd had with Joe.

Storm's father might have kicked her out, but he was out for blood. Little by little, he drained all money out of the Scott ranch. Angry, he wanted to go and squeeze the life out of Mr. McCrory. He lied and conned his father. He stole every asset on the ranch.

Guilt had Stetson sick to his stomach. He had caused the whole mess. Luckily, he'd made a killing as a rodeo star. He knew he had more than enough money to build this ranch back up for both him and Nellie. He planned to sign over half to her. If anyone deserved it, she did.

CHAPTER THREE

"That dreamy Stetson is back in town," Bailey said, walking into work almost an hour late. Putting her purse under the counter she looked at Storm and smiled. "Hey didn't you used to sleep with-- Oh, I mean date him?"

Instant rage flooded Storm. She wanted to grab Bailey's blonde hair and smack the oh so innocent look from her face. Instead, she put her tips in her apron pocket, gathered her stuff, and went into the kitchen to thank Frank, the cook.

Returning to the front of the diner, Storm was shocked to see Bailey giving Stetson a big hug. Pain lanced her heart as she watched. Being one of the top rodeo winners, Stetson's picture was constantly in their local paper, usually with a beautiful woman on his arm. Somehow, this cut deeper.

It was going to take all her courage to walk past them, and all of her acting skills to act as though she didn't care. How could she blame him for picking Bailey? She looked bright and young, not old and tired.

Storm needed to get out of there for no other reason than to get home to Scotty. Bailey had already made her later than usual. Keeping her head down, she passed by the couple only to have her arm grabbed. Stunned, she just stared at the large tanned hand holding her.

"Wait, I want to talk to you," Stetson said softly.

"I can't. I have to get home to Scotty."

"Oh my God! Stetson is the one who got you preggers?" Bailey asked, loud enough for the whole diner to hear. "Well, you probably don't know who the father is. Stetson, she isn't trying to rope you into being a daddy is she?"

Tears stung Storm's eyes as she struggled and finally freed herself. Once out of the door, she began to run. She knew she couldn't outrun the pain or the gossip, but she needed to be with her son.

Storm could see her house. Her feet throbbed and all she needed was a hug from Scotty. The crisp spring breeze had dried her tears. Damn Stetson, why did he have to come back? She'd been convinced her crying days were behind her.

She was almost there when she heard a truck coming up behind her. She didn't even need to look. She already knew who it was and she didn't want to talk to him.

Stetson drove past her and parked in front of her house. *He had some nerve*, she fumed, slowing down to a walk. Her eyes drank in the sight of him as he got out of his truck. His boots and jeans were dusty and his blue shirt looked wrinkled. He looked tired, almost as if he hadn't slept. Storm knew the feeling.

Shaking her head, she tried to draw from her hatred for him. It was inside of her. Looking at him made it hard to conjure up. Avoidance would be for the best.

"I need to talk to you."

"Some other time." Storm walked right by him.

"Storm, please?"

She refused to glance at him. She'd only give in. The door to her house opened and Scotty came barreling out. To Storm's consternation, he sailed right by her, and hurled himself into Stetson's arms.

*****

Stetson's heart soared as he picked up Scotty and held him close. He'd never felt such love before. Feeling Scotty's little arms around his neck opened his heart. Observing Storm, his heart squeezed. She appeared furious.

"Hi, Mr. Scott," Scotty said happily.

"Hey there, Scotty. Having a good day?"

Scotty laughed. "It just started silly. Mama is home."

Stetson glanced at Storm again and this time he could see her eyes tearing up. He never meant to cause her pain, but he had, big time. He'd heard the rumors and talk about her, and he didn't like it. Stetson knew they weren't true. Storm was a woman with integrity and a big heart. It seemed as though most of the town ignored that fact.

"I wanted to come by and ask your mother if she'd like to visit my horses." He wasn't playing fair, but damn it he wanted to spend time with Storm and his son.

"Yeah!" Scotty wiggled back down to the ground. Running up to his mother, he gazed at her with huge hopeful eyes. "Can we?"

Storm shot Stetson a glower of outrage. She peered down at her son, then back at Stetson. "Okay, only for a short visit."

"I'm going to see real horses."

"Scotty, run back in, and brush your teeth. I'll be right in," Storm told him, never taking her eyes off Stetson.

Stetson knew what was coming. He'd played unfairly. He just... God she was beautiful when she was mad. "Now, darlin', don't get mad."

"What did you call me? Listen, Mr. Rodeo Star, I am not yours or anyone's darlin'. You ruined my life. That is something I will never be able to put behind me."

"I—"

"I'm not done. Scotty is my son, mine. I believe he has a right to get to know you, but I lay down all the ground rules. This time it'll be me making the decisions that will affect my and Scotty's life."

Stetson could see the raw pain in her eyes. He wanted to tell her that he did try to see her the night he left. Her father had threatened to blow a hole in his head with the shotgun he held. He never told a soul about it, not even Nellie. He didn't want Storm to find out that her old man had sent him packing. He wanted to tell her now, but he could tell that she wouldn't be receptive to his explanations. He'd have to bide his time.

"I understand. We'll go by your rules," Stetson told her. He wanted to add 'for now', but he didn't dare.

"How long have you lived here?"

Storm stiffened. "Why? What's the matter with where I live?" she challenged.

"Not a thing."

Storm stared at him as if she was trying to decide if he was telling the truth. "I have to get changed. We'll be out in a few. Oh, and Stetson? I'll decide when and if to tell Scotty that you are his father."

Stetson watched her whirl around and go inside, slamming the door. *Damn*, he smiled, *she still lived up to her name*. She was a storm that blew the breath out of you. She'd always been that way. That's why he loved her.

*****

The ride to the Scott ranch was awkward to say the least. Storm kept glancing at Stetson, and when he looked her way, she turned her head. He sported a mustache and beard. It looked particularly sexy on him.

"Can I ride a horse, Mr. Scott?" Scotty asked.

"Call me Stetson."

Scotty smiled broadly and looked at Storm for

the okay. Storm nodded. "Okay Stez, Stets..."

Stetson looked down at Scotty's upturned face and grinned. "I like Stez. Finally a cool nickname."

Scotty looked so proud, it made Storm full of happiness. It was hard to stay mad when her son was so ecstatic. For his sake, she vowed to have a great day.

"Well? Do I get to ride a horse?"

"No."

"Yes." Stetson glanced at Storm as they answered at the same time.

"Scotty is too young."

"I'll put him in front of me. He'll be safe."

Storm nodded and looked away. She'd ridden with Stetson the very same way. She remembered the safety she had felt in his arms. Unfortunately, she also remembered how he kept kissing the side of her neck and sliding his hands under her shirt.

Her breasts grew heavy and her stomach felt as though the migration of the monarch butterflies were flying through it. Feelings she hadn't had since Stetson left. It had been a long time ago, she chastised herself. He had no interest in her that way anymore. He had money, he was famous, and she...

"What was that sigh for?" Stetson asked.

Storm knew the smile she gave him was a sad one, but she couldn't help it. "Nothing. Scotty is going to have a lot of fun here."

Stetson parked the truck and gave her a long look. He mesmerized her, but the memory of waiting in vain for him to come back to her invaded her being. Quickly, she glanced away and opened the door while Scotty tried to climb over her in his excitement.

Scotty got out and ran to Stetson. He was quickly scooped up into Stetson's embrace. Storm didn't know what to think or feel anymore. As much as she wanted to hate him, she couldn't. However, it didn't mean he had to be a part of her life.

The ranch appeared run down, and Storm was surprised. Observing the peeling paint and the general disrepair of the house made her wonder.

The front door opened, and Nellie flew down the steps. "Oh, Storm, I'm so glad you're here." She hugged her.

Stepping back, she looked at Scotty. "Oh wow, he's so handsome."

Storm felt overwhelmed by the warm welcome. She knew Nellie was the one who put the bags of clothes, food, and toys on her front porch. It had been too hard to take charity, but their little game of Nellie leaving them and Storm retrieving them, somehow made it okay.

"I want to thank you," Storm told Nellie.

Nellie reached out and squeezed her hand. "I don't know what you are talking about."

Storm squeezed Nellie's hand back and gave her a smile of thanks.

"Scotty, this is Nellie. She is Stetson's sister."

Scotty looked up and smiled. "Hello, Nellie."

"Pleased to meet you. Are you and my brother going to look at the horses?"

Scotty nodded. "Me and Stez are gonna ride like the wind!"

Nellie laughed. "Well, looks like the men are taken care of. How about a cup of coffee Storm?"

"I don't think— " she began.

"He's in good hands," Nellie said.

Storm swallowed and nodded. She tried to smile, but it just wasn't in her.

"I won't let anything happen to him," Stetson told her.

"Please, Mom?"

"Okay, kiddo. You do what Stetson tells you," Storm finally conceded.

"You betcha!" Scotty took Stetson's and pulled him toward the barn.

Storm watched them go. Her eyes misted.

"They'll be fine," Nellie said.

"I know." She couldn't seem to find an even keel. Stetson unbalanced her and she didn't like it one bit.

Nellie gave Storm a long look. Grabbing her hand, she led her inside. "I was going to offer you a cup of coffee, but I think a nap would be a better offer."

"I look that bad huh?"

Nellie shook her head. "Not bad, just tired. Come on, this big old house has too many empty bedrooms. Let's get you settled in one."

"Scotty might need me," Storm protested weakly.

"I think by now you know that I have Scotty's wellbeing in the forefront of my mind."

Storm smiled. "Yes, I do know. Thanks, Nellie, I could use some sleep."

"Last room upstairs on the right. You get some rest."

Storm nodded gratefully and headed upstairs.

*****

Storm woke up and for a split second, she didn't know where she was. She felt wonderful. She couldn't remember when she'd slept on such a comfortable mattress.

Getting out of bed, she realized that she could remember. It was before her father kicked her out of the house. Instantly she thought of Scotty, and immediately she was out the door. Walking down the steps, she heard voices. Hearing Scotty's name, Storm stopped to listen.

"I'm not going to let him go home to that dilapidated shack that Storm calls home," Stetson said, his voice sounding angry.

"Don't do anything you'll be sorry for. Storm has done the best she can by her son," Nellie defended.

"You call living in squalor, without enough food, her best? Nellie, get your head out of the sand."

"Stetson, you've been gone a long time. You have no idea what went on. You don't know how her father turned his back on her. Then our father discredited her claim that it was your baby. He made it his personal mission to make sure everyone knew that Storm didn't know who the father was."

"Obviously he's mine."

"Storm has been there for that child from the beginning. She has fought for everything they have. No one would give her a job. Do you think she wants to work the graveyard shift at the diner? It was the only job open to her."

"It's not enough. My son is not going back--"

Storm ran into the kitchen, glaring at Stetson. "Where is he? Where is *my* son?" She tried to quell her shaking body.

Stetson took a step toward her. "It's not how it sounded."

Putting her hand up in front of her, she signaled for him to stop. "I know exactly what I heard. Is that why you brought us out here? You plan to take Scotty away from me?" Tears filled her eyes. "I have done everything humanly possible to care for my son. He is fed and he has clean clothes. I provide him with a roof over his head. You have no right!"

Nellie stepped forward and wrapped her arms around Storm. "No one is talking about taking Scotty away," she said, rubbing her hand up and down Storm's back.

Storm allowed herself to be comforted for a moment, but she knew this wasn't the time. Stepping back, she looked first at Nellie then at Stetson. She didn't trust Stetson. Hadn't he hurt her enough?

"I would like to go home. Where is my son?" she asked, giving Stetson a look of defiance.

"He's napping. I put him in Stetson's room," Nellie told her. "Come on, I'll take you to him."

Storm pulled her attention from Stetson and nodded. She seethed inside, but now wasn't the time. Following Nellie upstairs, she found Scotty in a deep sleep.

He looked like a little angel. She was hesitant to wake him, but she had to get away from this ranch. She had to get him away from Stetson. Stetson thinking her a bad mother, cut deeply. He had no right.

Stetson's room smelled just like him, the fresh scent of the outdoors. She had never forgotten his scent. Many nights she had lain in bed, remembering every detail about him.

Hearing his footsteps, she stiffened.

"Storm?"

She could feel the heat from his body, but she didn't turn around.

"I'll take you home," he said.

Whirling around, she glared at him. "You will take us both home!"

Stetson nodded. "That's what I meant. I'd never separate you from Scotty. I know that's how it sounded."

"I know what I heard. I just want to go home."

*****

It had been a week since their awkward ride back to her house. All of his denials were for naught. She didn't believe him. Storm studied her watch for the hundredth time. Bailey was almost two hours late. Bailey didn't care that Scotty was home waiting. Bailey only cared about herself.

Scanning the parking lot, Storm watched Stetson's truck pull up. She wasn't in the mood for him today.

Everything had always been hard. Stetson made life harder. Curious, Storm watched Stetson get out of the truck and open the passenger side door. To her surprise, Bailey got out.

Storm's stomach soured. They were laughing and smiling. It looked like Bailey had him wrapped around her little finger. Yes, everything was harder since Stetson's return.

"Sorry I'm late." Bailey sailed through the door and went right to the cash register. Either they or Frank always counted the cash before each shift.

Storm refilled coffee for the customers, ignoring both Bailey and Stetson. She did notice he tried to catch her eye a few times, but she wasn't going to look at him. He didn't deserve her regard.

Storm returned behind the counter and grabbed her purse.

"Hey. Don't even think about leaving," Bailey told her.

"I need to get home."

"There's a hundred dollars missing from this register."

Storm felt the blood drain from her face. What was Bailey talking about? "Not possible. I counted it myself while I waited for you to show up."

"Frank! We have a big problem!" Bailey called the cook. He was part owner of the diner.

Frank turned the corner, wiping his hands on his food-splotched apron. "What's the problem now?"

"The drawer is short." Bailey walked up to Frank and put her hand on his arm.

"How short?"

"Frankie, there is one hundred dollars missing." Bailey's concern made Storm seethe.

Storm gaped at Frank. "I counted it a bit ago and it was all there. Maybe I should just recount it."

"Yeah, let's do that before we jump to conclusions." Frank smiled at Bailey.

"I'll do it," Bailey offered, brushing against the

counter and knocking Storm's purse to the ground. She knelt down to retrieve it. "Oh my, Storm, there's a hundred dollars here in your purse."

"No, that's not possible." Storm tried to grab her purse, but Frank got to it first. The whole diner was silent. She could feel their condemning eyes on her. "I didn't."

Frank sighed. "I'm sorry, Storm."

"I'm fired?" Storm held her breath hoping that someone would speak up in her behalf. She needed this job. Devastated, she grabbed her purse, minus the missing money and ran out the door.

"Storm!"

She knew it was Stetson and she willed herself to keep going, but suddenly she couldn't stand it anymore. Turning around she walked into his arms and sobbed.

Storm couldn't remember the last time she'd been hugged. Really hugged. Stetson's shoulders had always been wide, but somehow they seemed bigger, stronger. Closing her eyes, she took in his scent. He smelled of sandalwood, balsam, and mesquite. She breathed in again. Yes mesquite, though how he smelled like that she wasn't sure. She didn't care. For this moment, she wanted to enjoy being held.

All too soon, she became embarrassed. Stepping away, she gave him a quick, false smile and quickly glanced away. The pity she saw on his face shamed her. Wiping away her tears with the back of her hand, Storm turned and started for home.

She knew he'd follow her. Part of her was glad, but the sensible part just wanted to be alone to lick her wounds. It was colder than usual. The Texas wind felt biting. Shaking her head, she realized she had left her coat at the diner.

Bailey had set her up. That was the only explanation. Why Frank chose to believe Bailey over her, well what could she expect? Weariness washed over her as she continued to walk, her head down, straight into the wind.

"Storm, hold up!"

He followed her on foot; she was surprised he hadn't just jumped into his truck. Storm didn't stop.

Hearing his footsteps directly behind her, she turned around and tried to give him her best back off look. Of course it didn't work. "Stetson, I'm already over two hours late picking up Scotty. I don't have time to talk."

"Storm listen--"

"No! You listen! You brought that little tart to the diner two hours late. Then she counts the cash drawer and claims its one hundred dollars short? Oh yeah, did you notice the part where it was found right on the top of my purse?"

"I didn't--"

"I don't care if you did or didn't!" Turning toward home, Storm stomped off.

Stetson was next to her in an instant. "Did or didn't what?"

Storm's shoulder slumped and she sighed. Stopping she stared into Stetson's blue eyes. "It's none of my business who you sleep with. It's been a really long day already and I need to get home to Scotty." Tears poured down her face. This time she didn't bother to wipe them away.

Stetson's eyes narrowed. He appeared mad, but Storm didn't care. Let him be mad, she had more important things to think about, like where she and her son were going to live.

"Storm, will you just stop. I want to talk to you."

The look of pity was back in his eyes. "I can't, not now. I can't even wrap my brain around what just happened in the diner. I'm tired of being kicked like I'm some type of mongrel. My first priority is Scotty. I'd like to get home to him, alone."

Stetson reached out and cupped her cheek in his large work-worn hand. He seemed to be searching her eyes. Storm knew he'd find every emotion but defeat. "Okay, I'll call you later," he said, gently.

Nodding her head, she walked away. She didn't have a phone, but she wasn't about to tell him that. She could feel his eyes burning into her back as she walked away. Finally, she made it to the row of shanty houses. She had enough money for two more weeks. After that, she didn't know.

CHAPTER FOUR

The doorbell rang, and Storm shivered. Mr. Benson must have heard she'd been fired. He probably wanted his rent early. She witnessed it plenty of times before, whole families put out of their homes. Laws and mercy didn't seem to apply to her part of town. No one cared about those on shanty row.

Gazing around, she knew her furniture was on its last legs and the whole place was in general disrepair, but it had been her and Scotty's home since the day she brought him home. Reluctantly, she walked to the door. Her heart beat out of her chest. Where would they go?

Lottie Burns had graciously watched Scotty the last two days while Storm searched for work. A fruitless search. Half the people wouldn't even give her an application to fill out. She tried everywhere, Daley's General Store, Lasso Springs Feed Store, Lasso's Pizzeria, even the Whiskey Barrel Bar.

The only kindness she'd found was at Harriet's Yarn and Tea Shop. The usual ladies were drinking their tea. Harriett had rushed over to her and offered her a cup of tea and sympathy. She'd always been nice to both Storm and Scotty. She was a character though. Harriett was in her late sixties and wore a wig of waist-length black hair, which was usually askew. Storm declined the tea and pushed on.

Now her failure was going to result in them being homeless. Bracing herself for bad news, Storm opened the door. To her surprise it wasn't Mr. Benson, it was Nellie.

Nellie appeared too pale and her eyes conveyed distress. Storm took her hand and led her inside. Settling her on the couch, Storm ran to get some water. Nellie did not look at all well.

Handing her the water, Storm waited, wondering what was wrong. Her first thought was of Stetson. Maybe something had happened to him. "Nellie, tell me what's wrong?"

"Sit here next to me, Storm. I need you." Nellie's eyes filled with tears. One by one, they trailed down her wan face. "I don't know what to do."

"Tell me," Storm coaxed.

"Oh, Storm, I'm... well... I just saw Doc Benson."

Storm's heart raced. "What's wrong?"

"I'm pregnant. I just don't know what I'm going to do."

"Do?"

Nellie's eyes widened. "No, nothing like that. I need bed rest and I don't know how we're going to afford it. Stetson took off and--"

"He left?"

"Oh, not for good. He packed up his gear and rode out."

Storm closed her eyes and sighed. Nellie had been so very good to her over the years and now she finally had a chance to pay her back. "I'll come over every day and help you."

Nellie smiled. "I need a live-in person. I know you saw the state of the ranch. Only Joe Sullivan has stayed and well, we've done the best we could."

Storm watched Nellie blush when she mentioned Joe. "I don't think Stetson would want me there."

"Who gives a hoot what Stetson wants. I need you. He works all day anyway when he's home. You won't have to see him much."

Loud knocking interrupted the two women. Seeing Mr. Benson on the other side didn't fill her with terror. Not anymore. "I'm moving out today," she informed him.

*****

It seemed pitiful to Storm that all of her belongings fit in Nellie's car. Giving her neighbor and savior, Lottie a hug, she joined Scotty and Nellie in the car. It hadn't been the greatest of homes, but it had been filled with love. Storm's heart tugged as they drove away.

"Can't wait, can't wait, can't wait," Scotty chanted.

Nellie turned to smile at Storm. "Well at least one of you is excited."

Storm kept her hands on the steering wheel. "It's not that. I'm glad to be able to help you out. I hope that I'm able to take good care of you."

"You already are by driving. Don't stress, I have a feeling that everything will work out."

Storm glanced briefly at Nellie's stomach. "Who knows about..."

"No one yet. I'll tell Joe when we get home and as for Stetson, I guess I'll tell him when he gets back."

"How long did you say he'd be gone?" Storm asked.

"Three days. He has a place he goes, up on the ridge. He camps out up there. It brings him some peace. He always comes home in a better mood than when he left."

"It'd be nice to have a place to escape to for a while."

"Problems seldom go away by themselves," Nellie commented.

Storm nodded her head. "Don't I know it."

"Yeah! We're here," Scotty yelled from his seat.

A worried looking Joe came out of the house.

Nellie smiled at Storm. "Time to face the music."

"It'll be fine. I'll get you settled in and then Scotty and I will go down to the barn so you and Joe can talk."

Nellie seemed apprehensive, but she nodded.

Joe opened Nellie's door. The expression of concern made Storm envious. Joe would be there for Nellie, she could tell. Nellie wouldn't have to raise her child alone.

After dinner, Joe picked Nellie up and carried her to her new bedroom. They had decided a downstairs room would be the best.

Storm smiled. They were both wonderful people and Joe had asked Nellie to marry him. The earlier envy had faded and was replaced with happiness for Nellie.

"I know which room I want!" Scotty raced into the kitchen.

"Oh? And which room is that?"

"I want Stez's room. It has trophies, ribbons, and pictures of the rodeo. Can I, Mom?"

"Oh, honey. I don't think--"

"Tell him yes, until Stetson returns," Nellie yelled from her room.

"Yes!" Scotty raced up the stairs.

It hit her full force as soon as she walked into Stetson's room. The whole room was Stetson. There were trophies, ribbons, pictures, and belt buckles. Looking at the bed, she was glad they never made love there. It was bad enough seeing his things. Clothes were on the floor and she finally smiled. He never was a neat man.

"Now you know it's just for the night?"

"Yep, I'm going to bed now."

"It's early yet, kiddo."

"That's okay. Night, Mom."

"Fine, I know when I'm not wanted. I'll be up in a while to make sure that you've brushed your teeth."

Scotty just nodded to her.

Storm walked down the stairs and finished washing the dishes. She knew that she'd feel on edge until Stetson knew she was there. His reaction wasn't something she looked forward to. The front door opened and closed, and then Nellie called for her to join her.

"Joe's a good guy," She said, sitting in a chair next to Nellie's bed.

"Yes, yes he is."

"I'm happy for you."

"Thanks. Why Scotty?"

"Why what?"

"Why name your son Scotty? I mean there's nothing wrong with it. I just wondered."

Storm sighed. "Actually his name is Stetson Scott Jr. Your father came to the hospital after Scotty was born and threatened to take my baby away if I named him after Stetson."

Nellie's eyes grew wide. "He didn't. Oh God, Storm, you must have been frantic."

"It wasn't good timing. I missed your brother something awful. I also hated him for leaving me like he did. All the old biddies in town kept saying that I didn't even know who the father was. My father throwing me out fanned the rumors until people thought they were the truth. Your father made it a point to tell the world that my baby was not Stetson's."

"Oh God. I didn't know." Nellie's eyes grew misty.

"The next thing I knew, men were claiming that they had been with me. I don't know why. It crushed me."

*****

Stetson's heart hurt as he stood in the hall listening. If only he had stayed instead of running off to the rodeo circuit. Quietly, he went to his room. Seeing his son lying in his bed with his arm around one of his trophies left Stetson breathless.

Stetson just stared at Scotty. His whole heart expanded with love and thankfulness. He had a lot of making up to do. Both Scotty and Storm deserved better. He just hoped Storm would let him get close enough.

Stetson Scott Jr., Stetson couldn't believe it. Storm had named his son after him. The jab to his heart throbbed. If only... He had a ton of could've would've should'ves to last a lifetime. Regret ran deep within him. He really wished his father were still alive so he could beat the hell out of him.

He turned as Storm climbed the stairs. He winced at her expression of aversion. He wished he had the words to make everything better. He'd loved her so much once upon a time. Now he didn't even know her. They were different people.

"You're home."

"Yes, just a few minutes ago. Found a little munchkin in my bed."

Storm went to rush forward. Stetson grabbed her hand, halting her. "It's fine, Storm, really."

"No, it's your bed. I shouldn't have given in when he asked to sleep in it." Storm bit her bottom lip. "I can put him in another room."

"He's a handsome boy, isn't he?" Stetson asked, trying to distract her. "I'm glad you're here, both of you."

Storm gave him a long look and nodded. "It's just until Nellie is on her feet." Storm's eyes grew wide. She clamped her hand over her mouth.

"What's wrong with my sister?"

"I can't. Oh hell, you look like you're about to blow a gasket. I guess I had better tell you so we can get some sleep. I remember how persistent you can be."

"Come on." Stetson touched her arm. "Let's go into your room so we don't disturb our son." It hit him in the gut, he didn't know if he'd be a good father.

Stetson watched Storm's delectable rear end as she walked down the hall. He felt himself smiling. Stopping before entering her room, he studied her. "Now don't try to compromise me with your come hither eyes."

The alarm on Storm's face hit him full force. Stetson saw the hurt in her eyes before she turned away from him. She walked over to the window and watched as a thunderstorm rolled in.

"Appropriate weather," he commented.

Finally, Storm turned toward him, a sad smile on her face. "Life is so very complicated. Remember when we used to ride our paints across the plains? We were so young, so free, so happy, and now..." Storm turned to the window again.

"And now the father of your son doesn't know how to keep his big mouth shut."

Storm glanced over her shoulder. She looked surprised. "I'm used to it. I expect it at every turn, but I never expected it from you. We didn't come in here to talk about me or you. Nellie came to my house today, and said she needed me. Here I am."

Stetson's eyes narrowed. "Needed you for what?" He sat down on the bed, keeping his eyes on her.

"Damn! I knew you wouldn't settle for a vague story. I'll tell you, but you have to promise me that you will not yell at her or upset her in anyway."

Stetson nodded.

"Nellie is having a baby and she needs bed rest."

"What?" Stetson roared.

"Shhh. You'll wake Scotty and Nellie."

"You mean Stetson Scott the second?"

"Oh! You were listening in. That's not right," she whispered loudly.

Stetson got up and tried to brush past Storm. "What are you doing?" she asked, wrapping her arms around his waist.

"I'm going to talk to my sister."

"No you are not. You promised." Storm squeezed him hard around the middle until he groaned.

"Okay, just let me go."

"I don't trust you!"

The fight went out of Stetson. "That's our problem isn't, Storm? We don't trust each other."

"I have good reason not to trust you," she shot, letting go of him.

"If you say so. Good night. I won't see Nellie tonight, you're right. Joe's the father?"

Storm nodded.

"Okay then." He closed the door behind him feeling lonelier than he had ever felt.

CHAPTER FIVE

"Storm, you're going to wear a path in the rug with your pacing," Nellie admonished. "The guys will be back soon."

Turning, Storm gave Nellie a brief smile. "Of course, you're right."

"But you're worried."

"I know that Scotty is in good hands. I just wish that Stetson would have asked me first. Yelling 'we'll be back' means, we'll be outside. Not we're taking the truck and leaving for a few hours."

"They'll be home soon. I'm glad you're here. I'm feeling better already."

Nellie's kind words washed over Storm. It felt good to help someone out. "I'm glad. The color is coming back to your face."

Turning at the sound of a truck pulling up, Storm ran out the door to greet them. She'd smile for Scotty's benefit, but Stetson was going to hear it from her. He couldn't take Scotty whenever he felt like it.

"Hi, Mommy," Scotty shouted. He looked to be trying to carry something.

At the sight of the puppy, her smile faded. She

didn't want Scotty upset when they left. They wouldn't be able to take a puppy with them.

The little black dog squirmed in Scotty's arms. Scotty could barely hold it.

"I'll take him inside." Stetson rubbed Scotty's head, receiving a big smile from Scotty. He took the puppy into his big hands.

"Look what Daddy got me!"

Storm felt faint and her stomach churned. Daddy? What the hell?

Scotty gave her a great big excited hug. "I have a puppy."

Storm plastered a smile on her face, her mind whirling. How could Stetson have told Scotty? He had no right! She caught Stetson's gaze and she held it, hoping that he could see the daggers she sent him. The longer she stared the faster her heart beat. "Scotty, why don't you go show Nellie the puppy?"

"Aunt Nellie. She's my aunt, Daddy said so."

Her heart squeezed painfully. She almost doubled over. She watched Stetson herd both Scotty and the puppy into the house. Why? Had it been all a big plan? Nellie got them out to the ranch. Betrayal cut her soul. With long strides, Storm strode from the house. She needed to put distance between her and Stetson. She wanted to cry, scream, and slap Stetson. Would she ever be able to put to put her past behind her?

"Storm wait!"

Without missing a step, Storm continued walking through the Texas grass. There was no plan. She had no destination in mind. She was just fuming and had to get away.

Stetson's longer legs prevailed and he caught up to Storm. Her chest heaved when he took her arm and turned her toward him. "Storm..."

Her eyes misted. The last thing she wanted to do cry in front of Stetson again. Peering at him, her anger took over. Shrugging her arm out of his grasp, she took a step back. "How could you? How could you tell that little boy, my son, that you are his daddy? Good God, don't you think I should have been the one to make that decision? Did it occur to you that I wanted to be the one to tell him? You are selfish straight and simple, downright selfish!"

Storm turned and stalked away. She stopped after a few steps and turned to Stetson. "A puppy? Oh, you are pathetic. Don't you think that this is all hard enough without you trying to buy Scotty's love?"

Stetson's eyes grew wide and his mouth became grim. "I bought him that puppy because I wanted him to have it. I wanted to give him something. I've missed so much." He shook his head and put his hands in his pockets. "He asked me if I was his daddy. I wouldn't have told him if he hadn't asked. Of course it should have been up to you, but that's not how it happened."

"Nothing happens to go my way. I can see that's not going to change. Look, Stetson, I'm happy to help with Nellie, but after she's on her feet, Scotty and I are out of here."

"You'd take him?" Stetson asked heatedly.

"No, not like that. I will find us another place to live. I can't afford to move away from Lasso Springs. I would have left long ago if I could." Storm just stared at Stetson, trying to gage his honesty. "He just came out and asked if you were his father?"

"Yes, that's how it happened. We were in the truck and he blurted it out. I was shocked. It threw me, but I thought that honesty was the way to go."

She sighed as some of the anger left her body. "No, I mean yes, honesty is the best way. I just wanted to do it myself."

"He seems pretty happy about it." Pride was written all over his face.

"Well that makes one of us." Storm walked toward the house. Her feelings were too jumbled. Scotty must have questions and she wanted to be the one to answer them.

The sight of Scotty on the floor with his black lab puppy jumping on him and licking his face abated Storm's anger. Scotty's laughter was infectious. Before she knew it, she was on the floor with Scotty getting kisses from the new puppy. "So what shall we name him?"

"Daddy said that I can name him all by myself," Scotty answered excitedly.

"Did you think of one yet?"

"His name is Buck!"

"Are you sure you want to name him that? How about Oliver or Midnight?" Storm hoped he would change the name. Scotty had a hard time with his Bs and sometimes they came out as an F sound. Buck would end up sounding like...

Scotty lifted his chin in a manner that Storm knew all too well. He was digging in for a major stubborn streak. Storm glanced at Nellie who was smiling. It made no sense to upset everyone. "Well Buck it is. It's a fine name for a dog."

Scotty smiled. "I know, I already told ya that."

The door opened and Buck went flying, barking fiercely at Stetson. Storm smiled. What a good watchdog Buck was. She'd let Stetson deal with the mispronounced name.

"Daddy!" Scotty yelled, running up to Stetson. He was scooped up into his daddy's arms. "Guess what?"

"What?"

Scotty shook his head. "You have to guess."

Stetson focused on Storm apparently wanting some help. Storm ducked her head and bit her lip to keep from laughing.

"Well give me a hint."

Scotty shook his head looking very serious. "I'm just going to have to tell you. You'll need to work on guessin'. I named Buck. Buck!"

"Great name." Stetson put Scotty down and petted Buck.

"Ph-uck and me are gonna be friends!"

Stetson looked confused. "His name is Buck, right?"

Scotty rolled his eyes. "I already told ya that."

Stetson looked at Nellie, and then at Storm. They were both trying not to laugh.

"Scotty said that you told him that he could name the puppy." Storm stood up and grabbed two tissues, one for her and one for Nellie. They started laughing so hard that tears were streaming down their faces.

"But he's not saying Buck."

"He has a few little speech problems. He's only four you know. Sometimes his B sounds like F."

Stetson looked horrified.

"Don't worry, he'll probably grow out of it in a few years." Storm laughed and left the room. The mirth that bubbled inside her felt good.

She couldn't undo the past. She would do whatever she needed to do for Scotty's sake. She had a feeling she'd be biting her tongue, constantly. Hopefully, her heart could withstand the constant contact with Stetson. Part of her was attracted to him, but a larger part didn't trust him. Not with her heart.

*****

Dinner was lively. Scotty talked nonstop about his dog Buck. Stetson looked exasperated every time Scotty mispronounced Buck's name. So far, Scotty hadn't asked anything about why he hadn't had a daddy until now. Storm's mind whirled, trying to sort out what and when to tell him.

She watched Nellie and Joe gave each other long, loving looks. Once she glanced at Stetson and found him staring at her. She couldn't read his expression and wondered why he stared.

The doorbell rang and Storm jumped up to open the door. A sweet looking girl stood on the porch. Her chestnut hair curled wildly down her shoulders and her big brown eyes shone.

She looked at Storm and smiled. "I'm looking for Stetson Scott. He asked me to come for a visit."

A jolt of envy vibrated through Storm's body. This girl looked about 20 years old. Her complexion was all peaches and cream. Her clothes were ranch clothes, but they looked expensive on her perfect body.

Stetson joined her at the door. "Chrissy! What a surprise!"

Storm watched as Stetson smiled and Chrissy blushed. Her heart dropped. This must be Stetson's girlfriend. She felt pressure on her chest. Of course, he'd have a girlfriend. She should have guessed. Stetson, the famous rodeo star, lived here. For a moment, she had forgotten about his real life.

"Come in, come in." Stetson waved his hand in invitation. "I can't believe you're here."

Chrissy's smile lit up the whole house. "I came as soon as I could, just like I promised." She put her hand on his chest, stood on her tiptoes, and kissed him.

Storm glanced away. Their kiss brought out a side of her she didn't like. She went back to the table and sat down. Her plate was full, but she wouldn't be able to eat another bite.

"Well, get another plate and let the poor girl sit down," Nellie said.

Holding Chrissy's hand, Stetson led Chrissy to the table. Pulling out a chair, he urged her to sit down. "This is Chrissy, a friend from the rodeo circuit." He introduced everyone. The greetings were friendly but brief.

"He's my daddy," Scotty told her proudly.

Chrissy's eyes widened. She looked around until

she locked eyes with Stetson. "I had no idea."

Stetson placed a plate and silverware in front of her. He laid his hand on her shoulder. "It was a surprise to me too, sugar."

A lump formed in Storm's throat. Sugar indeed. She just hoped that Nellie was on her feet soon. If he'd only given her some notice. Hell, he hadn't even told her when he left five years ago. Why should she expect him to change now?

"Things at the rodeo just weren't the same without you, Stetson. I couldn't stay any longer. I missed you too much. I thought you would have returned before now. You did promise to be back soon."

"I've missed the circuit, but now I have a ranch to run."

"And a son to raise," Chrissy finished his sentence.

"That's a big enough reason to stay." Stetson reached out and ruffled Scotty's blond curls.

"I hadn't thought about starting a family so soon, but it'll be fun to have a little boy around."

Storm and Nellie shared expressions of alarm. What was going on? Was Stetson positioning himself to take Scotty away? Storm couldn't concentrate on the conversation around her. Her thoughts were all jumbled.

"Storm?"

Storm looked up and saw everyone watching her. "What?"

"Chrissy just complimented your cooking," Stetson told her.

Storm felt her face begin to heat. "Oh, um, thank you." She quickly glanced at her plate. She didn't want to look at Chrissy or Stetson.

"Wait until you meet ph-uck!" Scotty told Chrissy.

"That's not a nice word," Chrissy admonished.

Storm's eyes rose until she stared Chrissy down.

"I'll handle my son. He is saying Buck."

"No--"

Storm stood up before Chrissy could say another word. "Scotty, let's go out to the barn and collect Buck."

"Okay, Mommy! Bye, Daddy, bye Aunt Nellie, bye Joe, bye Sissy."

"It's Chrissy."

Storm ignored her and followed Scotty who was halfway to the barn already.

*****

Stetson watched Storm's retreat with misgivings. She was not pleased with him. Heck, he was surprised Chrissy had shown up at his door. He turned his attention back to the table. Every eye was on him. Joe glared. Nellie's eyes were wide with questions, and Chrissy looked at him adoringly.

"So, that's your baby mama," Chrissy said. "Wow, I bet it was a big surprise to you, Stetson. You have visitation with your son and the baby mama?"

Nellie gasped, then attempted to cover it with a fake cough.

"Baby mama? Have I missed something?" Stetson asked.

Chrissy smiled. "That's what they are called. She's not your ex-wife or anything. She's just your baby mama."

Stetson frowned. "That's disrespectful. Storm is the mother of my son. I don't want to hear the term baby mama again."

Chrissy frowned. Hell, she was good at making him feel guilty. "How's Brian?"

"He found a new girlfriend."

Stetson nodded. Now he knew why Chrissy had come. Her brother Brian was notorious for wanting the trailer all to himself when he had a new girl. Chrissy had bunked with him more than once. She'd always been a cute kid, but looking at her now, she was a woman. No wonder Storm skedaddled. "Does he know you're here?"

"Nope. He deserves to suffer. He should have kept better care of me."

"I'm going to get word to him."

Chrissy shrugged her shoulders. "Whatever. I'm not going back."

Stetson didn't reply. He'd learned over the years to ignore Chrissy's sulking. She'd just get her back up if he said anything. He saw the look of alarm on Nellie's face. He'd clue her in later, when he could talk to her alone.

"Well let's get your stuff and I'll show you where you can bunk."

"I'll just bunk in your room."

This time Nellie didn't try to cover her gasp. Stetson gave her a quick smile then turned to Chrissy. "No, you'll bunk alone."

Chrissy crossed her arms in front of her. "Is this because of your baby-- I mean, Scotty's mother?"

"Chrissy, you are my best friend's sister. There is no way you are bunking in with me. There are plenty of bedrooms."

Chrissy gave him another look of hurt. "I always bunk with you."

"At motels maybe, but not here."

"What?" Stetson turned and saw Storm at the doorway, Scotty and Buck by her side.

"We'll talk about this later," he said.

Suddenly Buck ran and grabbed one of Chrissy's flip-flops. He took off with it in his mouth. Tearing through the house, the yellow sandal looked bigger than he did. Storm and Scotty laughed while Chrissy threatened Buck's life. Finally, Stetson was able to grab the flip-flop from Buck. It had a huge bite taken out of it.

Sheepishly he handed it to Chrissy. He tried not

to laugh, but he couldn't help himself, especially when he heard Scotty's infectious laugh. Turning to Nellie, he noticed that she had her hand clamped over her mouth, her eyes full of merriment. Joe seemed to be just taking it all in.

"You owe me new sandals," Chrissy told Storm.

Storm held up her hands. "It's not my dog."

"Here's the other part of your phoe." Scotty held it out to Chrissy. "Maybe we can tape it." Scotty looked proud to have solved the problem.

"Like that's going to work!"

Watching Scotty's face crumble made Stetson's heart sink. Picking him up, he kissed Scotty's cheek. "I think it's a great idea, but I bet Chrissy would rather have a new pair of shoes."

Scotty nodded. "Bandit got new phoes."

"Bandit is a horse!"

"Now, Chrissy, don't get so bent out of shape. I'll replace the shoes. Right now I think I'll take Scotty and Buck for a walk."

Chrissy got up to follow.

"Get your gear and put it in one of the rooms upstairs. I'll be back in a bit." Stetson gave Storm a look that conveyed his apology, at least he hoped so. He didn't need two riled hens in his house.

*****

Busy making dinner, Storm enjoyed the quiet. Chrissy was talking to Nellie. She wasn't so bad. Storm got the impression she was spoiled and used to being the center of attention, Stetson's attention. Stetson's the one that stayed in hotel rooms with her. The thought really bothered her. He was free and single, and she had seen all the news stories about him. He always had a beauty on his arm.

Life goes on. Stetson did appear surprised when Chrissy showed up at the door. It was obvious by Chrissy's syrupy gaze she was in love with him. Stetson was too hard to read. He played it close to the vest.

Nellie was a joy to take care of. She asked for little. Storm gave her everything she asked for and more. It had been an interesting afternoon. Chrissy went out of her way to ingratiate herself to Nellie. She even fluffed Nellie's pillows for her.

Storm couldn't take her constant chatter. She was glad to have an excuse to leave the room. All she talked about was Stetson. Storm wanted to know what kind of brother throws his sister out when he has a girlfriend.

Hearing Scotty stir in his room above, Storm washed her hands. He was down the stairs before she could go get him. She heard him go into the family room. Following, she was surprised at Chrissy's angry voice.

Evidently Scotty had gone into Chrissy's room and found many flip-flops. He brought them down and dumped them on her lap.

"Bad, bad boy," Chrissy chastised, grabbing his arm.

Storm saw red. Instantly, she snatched her son away. He began to cry. Storm picked him up, but he cried louder and louder.

"Don't you ever touch my son again."

"Keep your brat out of my room."

Scotty wailed. "I want Daddy."

Storm led him out of the room, into the kitchen. "You shouldn't touch other people's things. You know that, don't you?"

Scotty nodded his head.

Storm put the lasagna into the oven. "Let's go out to the barn and find Buck."

Scotty smiled. "I want Daddy too."

Storm took Scotty's hand taking him outside. They saw Stetson walking toward them and Scotty was off running.

Stetson scooped him up and Scotty buried his face in Stetson's neck. Storm's worn heart flipped over. No matter what, Chrissy or no Chrissy, she needed to make sure that father and son had a relationship.

"What happened?" Stetson asked when Storm caught up to them.

"Scotty brought down an armload of flip-flops and Chrissy yelled at him."

"She hurted me, Daddy."

"What? Where did she hurt you?"

Storm took a deep breath. "She grabbed his arm and called him a bad boy and a brat."

"Daddy, are you going to punish her?" Scotty asked seriously. "This was really, really bad. She needs fifteen hundrethmill minutes in time out."

"Wow, that's a long time."

"I know, Daddy. She was bad."

"What about little boys who take things that don't belong to them? How much time do they get?"

Scotty scrunched up his face. "I think not much."

Stetson smiled. "Is that fair?"

Scotty looked sorry. "I only wanted to show her that she had other phoes. She was mean to Buck cause he ate her phoe. I showed her more phoes. Mommy only has two pairs and me only one."

Storm felt her face heat in embarrassment. They had what she could afford.

"I guess you have a point there, son. You can only wear one pair at a time."

"That's what I told you," Scotty told him, shaking his head.

Stetson looked over at Storm. "What was your reaction?"

He looked as though he was expecting the worst. "Don't worry, I didn't kill her. I just took Scotty out of her grip and told her not to touch him again. I don't know why you look surprised. Besides, I figure she's your girlfriend, you deal with her."

"Daddy has a girlfriend," Scotty giggled.

"She is not my girlfriend."

"You'd better tell her that."

"Daddy, put me down please. I need ph-uck."

Stetson put his son down and watched him run to the barn. "Talk about this later?"

"Sure," Storm called over her shoulder. She hurried to the barn.

CHAPTER SIX

It had only been a week, and Stetson didn't know how much more he could take. With three women, the house grew smaller and smaller. He never had a chance to be alone. The only happy people around seemed to be Nellie and Scotty.

Chrissy had taken to following him everywhere. If he went to check on the cattle, she'd saddle up a horse and come with him. If he decided to ride into town, she was at his truck before him. He'd always looked out for her while they were on the circuit, but this was different. She'd become a thorn in his side, but he couldn't be mean to her.

Damn her brother Brian. How he could take the responsibility of Chrissy lightly he'd never know. There hadn't been one woman that Brian had moved into his trailer worth the trouble. He'd always thought of Chrissy as a child, but she wasn't. All grown up and he could see it in her eyes. She had plans for him, for them.

He'd just have to tell it to her straight. Dread filled him. There would be tears for sure. Never for one second did he ever think he'd have to hurt Chrissy this way.

He hadn't had one single chance to get Storm alone.

He planned to spend the time she was on the ranch getting reacquainted. They didn't know each other anymore, but his heart told him that she was a major part of him.

Storm was all stirred up. Her parents correctly named her. She'd roll in suddenly in a mood to match his prize bull's. Then just as suddenly, she'd laugh. Mostly she laughed at him. She seemed to think it funny that Chrissy followed him around.

Stetson looked out at the yellow and orange colors come alive. Sunrise, it was the only peaceful time he'd had. A noise behind him made him sigh. So much for peace.

Scotty stood in his Batman pajamas, holding a squirming Buck. His bottom lip quivered.

"Hey, what's the sad look for?"

Scotty looked at Stetson with tears in his eyes. "Ph-uck is going to the pound. He doesn't mean it, Daddy. Please don't let that mean Sissy take my bestest dog away."

A lump formed in Stetson's throat. Chrissy hated Buck and Buck hated her right back. Picking up both Scotty and Buck, he kissed Scotty's forehead. "No one is taking Buck from you. I promise."

Scotty sniffled and wiped his nose on his sleeve. "But she said."

"I'll take care of it. What exactly did Buck do?"

"He bit all her phoes and piddled on them," Scotty wailed.

Stetson bit his bottom lip to keep from laughing. "How'd he get into her room?"

"I opened the door. Ph-uck wanted to go in. She snores really really loud."

"Well let's hope she's not too mad," Stetson said, putting Scotty and Buck down. "Let Buck out for a bit and go get dressed, okay?"

"Yes, Daddy. Promise she won't pound ph-uck?"

Stetson smiled at his son's worried face.

54

"Everything will be fine, Scotty. I promise."

Scotty looked at him for a bit then nodded. "Can I have a horse of my own?"

Stetson laughed. "Not today, but we can feed them together and then take a ride."

"I'll get ready," Scotty called over his shoulder.

Stetson shook his head. Scotty sure could run fast when he wanted to. He hoped that Chrissy didn't raise the roof when she saw her sandals. Stetson laughed. It was going to be a long day.

*****

Stetson and Scotty were already gone by the time Storm woke up. The disaster in the kitchen led her to the conclusion they had pancakes. Smiling, she poured herself a cup of coffee. Stetson had turned out to be a real hands-on father. He included Scotty whenever possible and it warmed her heart to see Scotty so happy.

She loaded a tray with decaf tea and crackers for Nellie. If only Chrissy would go home instead of hanging around Stetson all day. But so far, she hadn't shown any sign of leaving, especially without Stetson. Grabbing the tray, Storm started to walk toward Nellie's room. Chrissy ran right into her, causing the whole tray to fall. The tea splattered the walls and the cup shattered. Crackers flew everywhere.

"Where is he?" Chrissy demanded.

"Stetson is--"

"Not Stetson. Where is your brat and his gonna be dead dog?"

"Now wait a minute. Don't talk about my son like that." Storm glared at her.

"Well he won't be yours much longer. Might as well cut the apron strings now." Chrissy laughed. "Wow, you look surprised. Stetson is having the papers drawn up, and as soon as he does, we're out of here. Me, Stetson, and the brat minus one dog."

Storm felt her face drain of color. "What are you talking about?"

"How stupid can you be? The real reason I'm here is to help collect Scotty. Then we're going on to the rodeo circuit. Ever been? It's great fun and Stetson is a real champion."

"I don't believe you." Storm's heart began to beat faster and faster.

"Whatever. So where is that dog? I have a score to settle."

"With a puppy?"

"It's not your business."

"Everything that involves Scotty is Storm's business," Nellie told Chrissy. "I think it's best if you leave." Nellie looked worried and drawn.

Storm put her arm around Nellie's waist. "There's glass on the floor. Let me get you settled on the couch."

"Not until Chrissy gets it into her hard head that she's not welcome here."

"Whatever." Chrissy jerked the front door open and slammed it behind her.

"Now let me get you onto the couch. Good God, you're shaking."

"I'm just upset. She has no right speaking to you that way, Storm."

"I know, Nellie. She's lying anyway." Storm helped Nellie onto the couch. "I'll have your tea and crackers ready in a minute. Don't you worry."

Storm kept a fake smile on her face until she reached the kitchen. Grabbing the counter to keep from passing out, her mind whirled. What if Chrissy was telling the truth? Maybe she read the whole situation wrong. She had begun to assume that Stetson didn't want Chrissy here. Maybe he didn't want *her*.

It wouldn't be the first time she'd read him wrong.

What if Chrissy was telling the truth? They had been spending a lot of time alone together. Once a fool, always a fool. When would she ever learn?

*****

Stetson sighed in relief. He finally had a moment to himself. Most of his morning was spent refereeing the woman. He loved having Scotty and Buck follow him around, but his other shadow was wearing out her welcome. Chrissy had finally upset Nellie. That was hard to do.

Rubbing the back of his neck, he realized how tense he felt. He had hoped Chrissy would go back to her brother Brian on her own. He'd watched over her for the last five years and now he realized that she thought she had ownership of him.

Her cattiness was a side he had never seen before. He'd always thought of her as a sweet kid. Stetson shook his head. He should have realized that she had a crush on him. It simply never occurred to him. Chrissy had Storm and Scotty upset too. He had hoped that Storm was jealous, but he didn't get that vibe from her. She plain out didn't like Chrissy. He couldn't blame her.

Stacking hay bales helped to relieve his tension. Seeing a shadow coming toward him, he turned. Seeing Storm surprised him. Usually she avoided being alone with him. She looked much healthier than when she first arrived at the ranch. Her face had filled out and the dark circles under her eyes had disappeared. "To what do I owe the pleasure of your company?" He grinned at her.

Storm stared at him for a minute. She glanced away, as though she didn't know what to say.

"Did something happen?"

"This minute? No. I don't know where Chrissy is. Both Nellie and Scotty are napping together in Nellie's bed with Buck standing guard at the door." She gave him a half smile. "It's kinda cute actually."

Stetson wanted to tell her that she was cute too, but he didn't dare. "Well it's nice to have your company for a change."

"I have to talk to you." Storm looked as nervous as a cat in a lifeboat.

"Okay, spit it out. You're biting your bottom lip. I know something is wrong."

"Well, yes, maybe no." Her blue eyes stared into his. "It's just that Nellie is getting better and she won't need me, and I have to think about where Scotty and I are going to live. I won't let you take him on the rodeo circuit." Her eyes darkened.

Stetson raised his eyebrows. "The rodeo? Why would I take our son?"

Storm wrung her hands. "Chrissy told me that you planned--"

"Listen, if you have a question, ask me. Chrissy is not privy to my plans. Trust me enough to do the right thing."

Storm stared at the ground. "I don't know who to trust," she whispered.

Stetson stepped forward and put his hand under her chin, lifting her face to him. "Storm, trust me. I still don't know the whole of it. We were both lied to the day I left. I swear I came to tell you good-bye. I loved you, why would I have left without seeing you?"

She appeared so serious and then so sad. Her sadness went soul deep; Stetson could see it in her eyes. Leaning down he brushed his lips against hers. Her reaction wasn't what he expected. He thought she'd shove him away. Instead, she pressed her lips firmly against his.

A slight moan gave him hope. Pulling her into his arms, he relished her softness. No one ever fit him like Storm. When she opened her mouth for him, he thought he'd gone to heaven. Kissing her was like coming home. He'd been in the darkness and now he was stepping into the light. It took a minute before he realized that she was pushing at him.

Reluctantly he let her go. She looked beautiful, her lips ruby red and slightly swollen. The pain still shone in her eyes, making his heart squeeze.

"I have to go and check on things," she called over her shoulder.

Stetson watched until she went into the house. He wondered if the kiss was meant to give him hope or was it meant as a good bye?

"Sickening. The way she throws herself at you is so wrong."

Stetson turned to find Chrissy looking at him, her dark eyes flashing at him. "I don't want to talk about it and I don't like you spying on me."

"I just came out to see what you were doing. I didn't expect to find a make out session going on." Her eyes were practically bugging out of her head.

"Look, Chriss--"

Chrissy put her hand up. "I don't want to hear it." She turned and strode away.

Of course, she didn't want to hear it. He'd have to tell her to go eventually. He didn't want to hurt her. He'd get a hold of Brian and ask him to come get her.

He had to come up with a reason for Storm to stay on the ranch. That was going to take some thinking. She seemed to be able to see right through him. He couldn't lose her, not again. Hopefully he'd be able to make her see things his way.

*****

Storm leaned her back against the kitchen door. Touching her lips, she smiled. They kissed, and what a kiss it was. Every nerve in her body still hummed. *He left you. He left you.* She chanted hoping to find her anger.

Putting her hand on her chest, she could feel her

heart beating faster than it had in a very long time. It wasn't fair. She didn't want or need this attraction to Stetson. Why had he kissed her?

Hearing Nellie and Scotty singing in Nellie's room, she quickly went in to make sure that Scotty wasn't wearing Nellie out. They looked adorable; both still snuggled under a pink and yellow handmade quilt. There was no sign of Buck and Storm was immediately concerned. "Hey guys, nice singing. Have you seen Buck?"

Nellie caught Storm's eye. "He wasn't with you?"

"Oh no. I hope that she closed her door." Storm ran out of the room and raced up the stairs with her heart in her throat. Seeing Chrissy's door closed, Storm felt relieved. Thank God. She'd thought for certain that Buck had gotten into Chrissy's things again.

Suddenly Buck raced past with a pair of Stetson's boxers in his mouth. Storm didn't know whether to chase him or just laugh. They weren't her boxers. Hearing running and laughter Storm went back down to see the fun.

Nellie stood with her hand over her mouth, trying not to laugh. Scotty jumped up and down laughing hysterically and then there was Stetson trying to catch Buck. The thunderous look on Stetson's face didn't bode well for Buck.

Finally, Stetson caught up to the black lab and retrieved his boxers after a tug of war with Buck. Holding up his shorts, Storm was surprised at how big the holes in them were.

"Maybe Chrissy can mend those for you," she teased, smiling at Stetson.

Stetson shook his head. "This pup is a menace."

"Like Dennis?" Scotty asked.

"See, it's not so funny when it's your things being ruined by that monster," Chrissy said, entering the room. She stood there with her arms crossed, looking triumphant. "Good riddance to the dog."

Scotty looked at Storm with tears in his eyes. "Mommy?"

Storm knelt down and opened her arms to her son. He wrapped his arms around her neck and cried. Storm's heart hurt for him. "It's okay, kiddo. Buck isn't going anywhere."

"How dense can you be?" Chrissy demanded. "That dog is no good."

"Enough. Can't you see that you're upsetting Scotty?" Storm picked him up and rocked him back and forth. "I promise. Daddy isn't mad at Buck."

Stetson finally smiled. "It's all right, bud. I shouldn't have left my stuff on the floor. Buck was just playing."

Scotty stared at him and finally nodded. "Okay, Daddy. Mommy, can we take ph-uck for a walk?"

"Let's get your eyes dried off, and then we'll go." Storm set him down and kissed the top of his head.

Scotty took the bottom of his shirt and brought it up to wipe his face. "Ready."

"Nellie will you be fine if we go?"

Nellie smiled. "Go on. Stetson is here if I need anything." She blushed. "I'm expecting Joe any minute."

"You'll be in good hands." Storm helped Scotty gather Buck and they were soon out the door.

*****

It had been hard keeping Scotty and Buck away from Chrissy. Her dislike seemed to draw them to her for some reason. Storm kept waiting for Stetson to send Chrissy home, but it had been almost a week since Stetson had kissed her and Chrissy was still here.

Joe planned to take Nellie in for her doctor's appointment, leaving Storm free to do what she wanted. She wanted to ride. It used to be she'd ride more than she walked. Used to be. There seemed to be several used to be times in her life.

It had been busy on the ranch lately. Stetson had hired men to fix the barn and the house. A few new horses graced his stable. The gentlest one was Mitzi, a freckled Appaloosa. Scotty loved all of Mitzi's brown spots and he practiced counting by trying to count her freckles. Storm loved her silky blond mane.

"Ready?" she asked Scotty, who had patiently waited for her to saddle the horse.

"Ride 'em cowboy!"

Storm laughed. "It'll be fun to see some of the ranch."

"I've seent it with Daddy. One day it be my land."

Storm wasn't so sure about that. She lifted Scotty up and had him hold onto the saddle horn. Putting her leg into the stirrup, she maneuvered herself right behind him. "Hold on tight."

"Wheeee. Hi ho silver!"

Storm laughed. "Now where'd you hear that?"

"Aunt Nellie told me to say it when I'm on a horse."

Storm felt instant serenity, riding across the ranch. Spring had finally come to Texas. Red and yellow Indian blankets, yellow Texas stars, and white fragrant lilies covered whole areas. It provided a spectacular view.

The cattle they saw looked healthy, though the number was few. She wondered what had happened to the Scott ranch. She hadn't heard anything, but then again most people didn't talk to her.

Riding to the fence that separated the Scott's property from her father's, Storm just stared. He father had an abundant amount of cattle roaming the land. He was a wealthy man. It hurt to look at the place that used to be her home. Quietly she turned Mitzi around and headed back.

"Nothin' like the wind on the face," Scotty told her.

"Stetson tell you that one?"

"Yep."

Storm's heart warmed. She loved their special bond. She had been jealous at first, but seeing how happy it made Scotty, she encouraged the relationship.

"Is Chrissy going to go home?"

"Where did you hear that?"

"I told her to," Scotty said, proudly.

Storm bit her bottom lip. She didn't know whether to laugh or be alarmed. Chrissy acted like a nut job half the time. "What did you say?"

"I said, you go home. This will be my land and I make the rules."

"Oh?"

Scotty nodded, still holding on to the saddle horn.

"Well, kiddo, I don't think that you do make the rules."

"I will someday," he replied, stubbornly.

"I doubt she has left. Don't tell her to go again. It makes her mad."

"Okay, Mommy."

Storm hoped that psycho Chrissy hadn't been upset by Scotty's words.

*****

With her legs aching, Storm brushed down Mitzi. It had been too long since she had spent time in a saddle and her whole body felt it. The ride with Scotty had been incredible. He took such an interest in his surroundings.

She wanted to laugh about Scotty's dictate for Chrissy to go home, but she had a sneaking suspicion that Chrissy would use it to her gain. Somehow, she always turned things to her advantage.

"Mommy! Mommy!"

"In here, kiddo." Storm immediately put the curry brush down and settled Mitzi in her stall.

Scotty's tears fell freely down his face. He flung

himself at her. His heaving and sobbing made it hard for Storm to make sense of what he was trying to tell her.

Scotty sniffled and looked at Storm. "She got rid of Ph-uck. She had no right! Ph-uck is in doggie heaven!"

Storm's heart lurched. The heartbreak on Scotty's face made her hurt for him. "Who got rid of him?"

"Sissy. She, she, Ph-uck is never coming back. Mommy, he's my ph-estest friend."

"I know he's your best friend, honey. Let's go and see what's up." She stroked his blond curls, then kissed his cheek.

Storm carried her distraught son across the yard. There must be some mistake, some explanation. Setting Scotty on one of the porch chairs, she told him to stay there. She wanted to confront Chrissy herself and hear it from the horse's mouth.

Chrissy smiled at her looking mighty please with herself. "Did Scotty go and tell on me?"

"You slack-jawed pole cat! Pick on someone your own size. Where is Buck?"

"Slack-jawed? At least I can pronounce Buck's name."

"Oh wow. You just equated yourself with a four year old. You're pitiful, and I am fed up with you treating my son meanly. You just hush your mouth for now on."

"Fine, well I reckon that you don't want to know what happened to that dog. You should be nice to people you want answers from." Chrissy wrapped a strand of hair around her finger and smiled.

"Where is Stetson?"

"Why do you want to know? He doesn't want anything to do with the likes of you. I don't know why you don't just take your brat and leave."

Storm felt as though steam was coming out of her ears. She couldn't remember ever being so mad. "You listen to me, and listen good. That dog had better be alive or I will hunt you down and shoot you myself."

Chrissy looked as though she was enjoying every

minute of their conversation. "That's trash talk, but I guess that's what you are. You're never going to be more than an ignorant country bumpkin."

Joe hurried into the room observing one woman, then the other. His eyes narrowed when he zeroed in on Chrissy. "What's this I hear about Buck being dead?"

Chrissy smiled at him.

Joe took a step toward her. "That dog better be safe somewhere. Now start talking."

Shrugging her shoulders, Chrissy nodded toward the door. "He went that way. Makes no never mind to me whether you find him or not. I did everyone a favor."

"Nellie will stay with Scotty. Let's get busy looking before it gets much later," Joe said, giving Chrissy a look of disgust.

"Is Nellie able to watch him? He's really upset."

"She's good to go. Doc said she's fine. Let's go."

Storm gave Chrissy one last glower of loathing, and followed Joe out of the house.

Joe and Storm looked in every nook and cranny near the house and barn. There was no sign of Buck. Storm's heart grew heavier with each passing minute. Black clouds rode in, and they didn't look friendly.

"I'm going to saddle Rosie and take a gander," she told Joe.

"I should go. You stay."

"We might as well both go. We can cover more ground. I don't know about you, but I don't relish walking back into the house without Buck."

Joe nodded. "Let's get saddled and ready to go. I don't like the look of those clouds."

"A little rain won't hurt us." Storm hoped her words to be true.

Joe stopped her before she mounted up. "Be careful. You have your radio with you?"

"Yes."

"Keep it on. Don't go too far out."

"Good advice." They both mounted up and rode in different directions.

The wind started to kick up, and the temperature seemed to drop. Storm searched and searched. What was she supposed to tell Scotty? Where was Stetson? She'd forgotten to ask. It wasn't as if she was his wife or anything. Nothing in fact. He didn't have to report his whereabouts to her. Heading toward the creek, Storm thought she spotted something on the small little piece of land in the middle of the creek. She wasn't sure what made one thing a creek and another a river, but this looked more like a river to her.

Damn, Buck was stranded on the island. How the hell? She didn't even have to finish her thought. She already knew. Dismounting from Rosie, Storm grabbed her rain gear. It was only a waterproof poncho, but it usually did the trick.

The heavens opened and torrential rains came down. It was a gully washer for sure. Getting back on Rosie, Storm attempted to ride Rosie through the creek. Rosie wasn't having it. She planted her hooves and refused to move.

Buck was barking and whining, pulling at her heartstrings. She'd wade over and back. Getting wet wouldn't kill her.

Searching for a spot to cross, Storm found a fallen tree that spanned the length of the creek. She had no illusions that she'd be able to cross it on foot. Co-ordination was not one of her talents. Grabbing the log to guide her, Storm waded into the creek. It started rushing faster. It's a river, she swore to herself. It took a lot of strength to hold on to the tree and make her way across. She swore at Chrissy the whole way.

Finally, she reached the other side, but Buck had disappeared. This was not her day. The island was tiny, but it was blanketed with low brush. Hearing a bark, Storm finally found Buck and quickly took him into her weary arms.

They were both soaked due to the deluge of rain. When it rained in Texas, it really rained. Storm made her way back to the fallen tree only to find it had washed away. "This is not a creek." She looked at Buck. "I'm telling you it's a river. A big old nasty, deep, fast running river."

Her boots were soaked along with her socks. Miserable, that's how she felt. Damn that Chrissy. Looking up at the sky, the clouds looked even darker. A bolt of lightning sent Rosie racing away. "What do you think Buck? Laugh or cry?"

Buck whined. "I'm with you on that. Things could be worse. I have a piece of gum in my pocket. See Buck, there is a bright side."

The lightening was fierce, followed by booms of thunder. She'd have to wait it out. Taking out her radio, she examined it. It was wet too. Finding a stump under a canopy of tree branches, Storm sat and snuggled Buck to her. All she could do was wait.

She couldn't help but jump as the big dark sky lit up. She finally saw a rider in the distance, leading Rosie behind his horse. She could tell by the way the rider sat that it was Stetson. The cavalry had arrived.

He rode closer and Storm could tell that he was not pleased. His mouth was a tight line. He looked like he wanted to lecture her.

"Oh, good you found me," she yelled, trying to sound cheerful.

"What are you doing?"

"Looking for your son's dog that your girlfriend tried to kill." She could tell by the murderous look in his eyes that he was not happy with her answer.

"I heard Buck got loose."

"Yeah, right, and he swam over here too."

Stetson swung down out of the saddle and looked the creek over. "How'd you get over?"

"I waded. A tree had fallen and I held on to it, but it's

washed away."

He sighed. "Yeah, a real gully washer. How did you plan to get back?"

"Oh for goodness sake Stetson, just get me home!"

Stetson finally smiled and Storm had a sneaking suspicion that he was trying not to laugh. "I'll come get you."

"It's not safe."

"Don't get your knickers in a knot."

Storm held her breath, watching Stetson wade into the creek. His eyes widened when he felt the rush of the water. A couple times, she thought he'd be washed away, but finally he made it. He was soaked through.

"Didn't you have any rain gear?"

"Obviously not. Now tell me again why you and Buck are here?"

Storm went back to the log she had been sitting on. "Might as well get comfy, we can't go back until the river slows."

"Creek."

"Oh, who cares? Personally, I think it should be called a river. Sit."

Stetson sat beside her and took Buck into his arms. "Out with it."

Shaking her head, she grew angry. "You make it sound like it's my fault. Scotty and I took a ride on Mitzi. When we got back, Chrissy said she got rid of Buck. Of course, Scotty was heartbroken. He thought his best friend was gone."

Stetson nodded, looking out across the creek.

"Nellie and Joe came home from the doctors -- she's fine by the way -- and Joe and I decided to look for Buck."

"You think Chrissy put Buck here?"

"Get your head out of the sand, Stetson. She told Scotty that Buck was in doggie heaven."

Stetson ran his hand over his face. "Awe hell, and she's not my girlfriend."

Storm laughed. "Does she know that? It seems to me that she has future plans for you."

"Not funny."

Storm grew serious. "No, it's not. Not when she pulls stunts like this. Scotty is beside himself and Joe might be caught in the storm."

"Joe's fine. He answered his radio."

"Mine got wet."

"I figured, but when I came across Rosie, it scared the hell out of me. I thought you'd taken a fall."

A budding warmth entered her heart. "You were concerned about me?"

"Well I didn't want to tell Scotty his mother was hurt."

So much for warm and fuzzy. He wasn't concerned about her as a woman, just as a mother. Somehow, it felt depressing. "I want you to talk to Chrissy about this stunt."

Stetson studied her. His eyes full of concern. "Don't worry, I called her brother. He's coming to get her. Look, Storm, I'm sorrier than I can say about her. I never meant.... Hell, my priorities right now are my family and the ranch."

Storm wished she were part of that family. Somehow, she felt more alone than ever. "Nellie and Scotty should be your first priorities."

"You're part of the family too, Storm."

She glanced away without acknowledging his comment.

They heard static from his radio. He dug it out of his pocket. "Forgot to radio Joe I found you."

"He's bound to be worried."

Stetson nodded. "Joe, found her and Buck. We are on Sinner's Island."

"What are you doing way out there?"

"Water's too high. Can't cross back till morning at the earliest."

"I'll bring you some supplies. Need dry clothes?"

Joe asked.

"Warm clothes."

"See you soon, buddy."

"Thanks, Joe."

Stetson smiled at Storm. "Well, we won't be stuck here indefinitely."

"Oh is that supposed to be the bright side? As far as I'm concerned anytime alone with you is a hardship."

"I do believe that you are fibbing."

Storm's eyes widened. "Fibbing?"

"Yes. Fibbers never win."

Storm shook her head. "That's quitters never win."

"Really?"

"Stetson Scott, you are the most infuriating man. You are making fun of me. Well go ahead, it's nothing I haven't heard before."

Stetson grew serious. "No, Storm, I only meant to tease you. I'd never make fun of you."

Storm shifted on the fallen log and turned away.

"It was bad when I left."

Storm nodded her head, but she didn't turn toward him.

"If I had known. Storm, I would have stayed. I loved you heart and soul, and it was the hardest thing I've ever done, leaving you." Stetson took a deep breath. "I was there that night. I went to tell you. I hoped you'd come with me."

Storm jerked around and stared at him. "If only that was true, but it's not. The truth hurts, but at least it's the truth."

"No, Storm, none of what we were told was the truth. Too many secrets have ruined our lives." He reached over and brushed an errant tear off of her cold, wet, cheek.

Storm shivered. "Oh your hands are cold."

"Oh yeah? How about this?" Stetson reached under her rain poncho and ran his cold hands under her shirt, across her bare back.

Storm screamed and squirmed. Buck barked wildly. "Stop, please," she squealed again. "Stop."

Stetson didn't stop. He looked into her eyes. Pulling her closer, he leaned toward her to kiss her.

Storm screamed as all the water that had gathered on his hat, poured on her face. She sputtered and stared at him, her mouth open in surprise.

Stetson laughed hard. The next thing he knew, her wet, freezing hands were on his bare abdomen, causing him to jump back. Storm jumped with him. "I'm sorry, Storm."

"I bet you are now," Storm laughed, climbing on his lap, moving her hands up to his chest. Her realization of what she was doing seemed to dawn on her. Her eyes widened and she began to push away.

"Storm," he growled, pulling her close, her hands trapped between them and she shivered. "Cold?"

"Yes, so let go."

Stetson pulled back a bit and searched her face. "Is that what you really want?"

Storm bit her bottom lip.

Leaning in, his lips found hers, kissing her. Storm groaned as he nipped at her bottom lip until she opened for him. "Stetson."

"Shhh." He continued to kiss her.

"Stetson."

Stetson came up for air "What?"

"Joe's here."

"Oh hell."

Storm laughed as she felt the reason for Stetson's discomfort against her. His arousal couldn't be hidden. "The rain will cool you off," she teased.

Stetson grabbed her in a bear hug, kissing her neck. He stood up with her in his arms, kissing her again. Finally, he set her down and went out from the canopy of trees into the pouring rain to meet Joe.

"Great timing," Joe yelled smirking.

"Thanks. How are you planning to get the stuff over?"

"A pulley system -- almost like a zip line."

"Clever, Joe. Thanks for the rescue."

Joe sent over a tent, sleeping bags, dry clothes, and food. It took a while, but finally he was done. "Scotty says he sorry you got yourself marooned on a desert island."

Stetson laughed. "Tell him we love him. We should be able to get back across tomorrow."

"I'll call you on the radio and come get you."

"Thanks, Joe."

"Stay warm." Joe gave Stetson a wink and walked away.

Storm felt as though she had the devil on one shoulder and an angel on the other. Her thoughts were warring against one another. The kiss was amazing. Stetson had the power to send chills up and down her body. He electrified her.

Turning away from him, she tried to compose herself. Her body ached with desire. It had been so very long and she wanted him with all of her being. Mentally shaking herself, she knew that it couldn't happen. It wouldn't happen. Stetson had been her whole world once, and her world combusted.

"That's a lot of stuff Joe sent over," she commented, finally turning around to face Stetson. He didn't show any emotion on his face and it made her wonder if the kiss meant anything to him.

"A tent, sleeping bags, and warm clothes. We'll be fine."

"Shouldn't we make a fire?"

Stetson smiled. "The wood is too wet. We'll make do with our body heat." His eyes looked too innocent.

Narrowing her eyes, she watched him. He looked pleased about something. "What exactly do you mean about body heat?"

"We have to share to keep warm." He took the tent out of the waterproof bag and began to set it up.

"That tent looks awfully small."

Stetson laughed. "Big enough for me and Buck."

"All right, I get the message. How can I help? Want me to hold a pole or something?"

"As much as I appreciate the offer, I do this alone all the time. Why don't you grab Buck before I trip over him."

Storm picked up the black lab and cuddled him. "This will be my first time away from Scotty. Well, except for work. I hope he's not upset."

Stetson stopped and walked over to Storm. He kissed her on the cheek. "You are a good mom." Before she could reply, he went back to work.

Storm's heart fluttered. It wasn't something that she heard very often. Her eyes misted. Maybe he did come to tell her goodbye.

Stetson disappeared inside of the tent, taking in the rest of the supplies. A few minutes later, he came back out and looked at the sky. "Darkness will be here before we know it. Best get settled in the tent while we can see."

"I feel like a drowned rat."

"I'm wet to the bone too. Get inside, take off your clothes, and get into the sleeping bag."

He looked serious, but Storm knew that he had to be kidding. "Good try cowboy, but this here gal doesn't get into sleeping bags naked."

"Oh for Pete's sake. Joe didn't pack you a nightie."

"What about the warm dry clothes?"

"Those are for tomorrow."

Storm looked at him long and hard. "All right. We'll do it your way."

Storm crawled into the two-man tent. Quickly she got out of her wet clothes and flung them out the door. Buck jumped all around having a great time. "Chew on Stetson's shoes not mine, okay?" She told him.

Looking at the sleeping bags she discovered that they were zipped together to make one big sleeping bag. "Stetson."

The rain had stopped, and the sun had set. The whole world seemed wet and damp. "Storm?"

"What?" Storm called.

"I was kidding. Get dressed. I'll be right in."

Storm frowned. His words sunk in and she grew hopping mad. Kidding? Kidding? If she could lock the tent door, she would. Scurrying out of the sleeping bag, she grabbed her dry clothes. Chrissy must have packed them. Her oldest panties with holes in them were there, as was a shirt with a stain. Storm put them on as quickly as she could.

Back in the sleeping bag, she watched Buck romp around, attacking her feet as she moved them. She was mad. Well, part of her was disappointed too. There had been so many long lonely nights when she craved Stetson's arms around her, shouldering some of the burden.

The woman in her wanted that sexy cowboy. She wanted to stroke his beard and kiss his neck. She wanted to put her hands on his hard muscled chest. Shaking her head, she willed herself to think of something else. Unfortunately, it didn't work.

Hearing Stetson unzipping the door to the tent, Storm turned away from him. Let him get naked, she didn't care. He could stand on his head singing the Star Spangled Banner, naked, and she still wouldn't care.

The rustling of his clothes equated to nails on a chalkboard, making her cringe. Every one of her senses seemed to be in overdrive. She felt hypersensitive. Trying to block him out didn't work. Her hands hung tightly to her side of the sleeping bag in an attempt to resist the temptation to turn and see him.

"What's taking you so long?" she asked crossly.

"Impatient to have me in your bed?"

Storm could hear his humor and she didn't appreciate it. "I just want to get some sleep is all."

Stetson laughed a deep rumbling laugh. "You sure are as skittish--"

"Don't you dare compare me to one of your animals."

The lack of response confused her. She could feel Stetson slide into the sleeping back and she tensed, waiting for him to draw her close. She planned to put up a token resistance and then give in. God help her, but she needed that man to love and cherish her.

What was he waiting for? She heard him murmur to Buck, then silence. What type of game was he playing now? It had her shaking in need. Finally, she couldn't stand it anymore and just as she was about to turn to confront him, she heard a loud snore.

Rolling onto her back, she stared at the tent ceiling. Disappointment washed over her, pouring into ever crack and crevice. Whenever she forgot for a second who and what she was, she got hurt. She wasn't good enough for Stetson Scott, Rodeo Star. Her heart felt split open. It had never quite healed from the first time Stetson had left her. A lot had happened since, but the hurt was still there. She was too vulnerable where he was concerned.

Nellie was feeling better. It would be wise to look for another job. Who would hire her? Another part of her heart cut open. Her father had made sure that she wasn't hired by anyone. She didn't wonder what she had done to bring down the wrath of both her father and Stetson's. She'd wondered for five long years and it got her nowhere.

Storm suddenly felt weary. Closing her eyes, she slept.

A sonic boom of thunder shook the earth and the sky was luminous. Star jumped at another round of thunder. Buck began to whimper. Sitting up, Storm grabbed up the puppy and murmured to it.

"You're going to squeeze the stuffing out of Buck."

Stetson's masculine voice shrouded her, making her

feel safer. Lightning flashed again and Buck jumped from her arms to Stetson's. Storm didn't blame him. Huddling under the sleeping bag, she began to shiver. Turning her back to Stetson, she huddled down so that her head was covered.

"Can you breathe?" The humor in his voice didn't help her mood.

"I'm fine."

"Are you sure? It's just as safe up here in the air."

"You won't act improper will you?"

Stetson laughed. "Improper? Listen, you've made it clear that you don't want me touching you. We don't have that type of relationship. We just happen to have the same son."

It's what she wanted all along, wasn't it? Now she wasn't so sure. "Well that's a relief."

"What?"

Storm sat up and looked at him. Every so often, the lightning illuminated his handsome face. "I'm glad we finally agreed that our relationship is only for Scotty's sake. Anything else, well, I just couldn't."

Seeing the frown on his face gave her pause. She knew it was for the best. They could barely tolerate each other and she didn't want Scotty to know.

"Listen," Stetson said.

Storm smiled. It had stopped raining, the clouds had moved on. The peacefulness was soothing. That's what she wanted for their relationship, peace. "What time is it?"

Stetson grabbed a flashlight and shined it on his watch. "A little past one. We might as well try to get more sleep."

Storm nodded. "Might as well." Turning her back to him, she felt a pang of regret. She could love him, if she allowed herself, but self-preservation had become a habit with her out of necessity. She had to think about Scotty first. It wouldn't be good for him if his parents came together only to split up. There had been too much hurt already.

So that brought her right back to the beginning. Nellie was well now and she didn't need her anymore. She had to find something to support her and Scotty. It would have to be something in town since she didn't have a car. She racked her brain trying to think of a place she had missed in her job search, but nothing came to mind.

Besides, she was certain Bailey had told the whole town she'd been fired for stealing. As if her life could get any lower. Well, if Bailey expected to win points with Stetson, it hadn't worked. He spent his evenings with Scotty.

Storm smiled as she thought of the two of them. Both acted as if they were four. The love between them made her heart warm. She was confident Stetson didn't plan to take Scotty away from her. She wondered what the future held, probably family gatherings with Stetson and his wife and kids -- if he had any. The thought of having to endure such a thing made her shudder. It also made her extremely sad.

Kathleen Ball

CHAPTER SEVEN

It had been a rough morning, packing up all the gear and getting it back across the creek. Thankfully, the water levels had gone down and they easily got to the other side. Joe had been waiting for them.

Going across the prairie, they were jostled and bumped in the truck. Storm sat in the middle and he wanted to laugh at how hard she was trying not to touch him. She was losing the battle.

"So, Scotty wasn't upset?" Storm asked for the fourth time.

Joe didn't take his eyes off the land before him. "He's fine. Had a great time with Nellie and me."

Storm didn't look convinced. Frowning, she crossed her arms in front of her. Maybe she didn't believe Scotty could have fun without her.

Stetson looked out the window. It wasn't fair. He knew she was anxious to see Scotty and he understood her worry. He had two things on his mind. One was to hug Scotty and listen to his adventure of being brave without them. The second was to confront Chrissy. He looked at Buck. He was such a sweet, black lab. How could she have left him on Sinner's Island? It would have been a death

79

sentence for the little guy if Storm hadn't found him.

It was time for Chrissy to move on. Way past time. He should have told her to leave long ago.

Storm began to squirm next to him. Looking up, he saw Scotty and Nellie waiting for them. Scotty pulled away from Nellie's hold and ran. "Stop the truck; we have one excited cowpoke coming our way."

Storm practically climbed over Stetson, trying to get to her son. Tears streamed down her face as she opened her arms to him.

Scotty quickly ran to his mother and wrapped his little arms tight around her neck. It wasn't a long hug. Scotty let go and wanted Buck.

He ran and grabbed the wriggly dog into his arms. He smiled at Stetson and started for home. Stetson felt robbed. Where was his hug? He could see Storm looked just as bewildered as he felt.

Putting his arms around her, he gave her a light squeeze and let go. She nodded in appreciation and they both walked into the house.

"Oh man, Ph-uck was so lost! Ph-uck was you scared? Did you get wet? Did you miss me?"

Soon enough they were both on the braided rug in the family room rolling around together. Stetson couldn't remember a more heartwarming scene.

Scotty stopped and looked at Stetson with big blue eyes. "I thoughted he was deaded. He never goes anywhere without me." His bottom lip quivered. "Do you think he runned away from me? Maybe I'm not his bestest friend."

Watching Storm, he could see her sorrow for her son written all over her face. Scooping both Scotty and Buck up, he sat on the couch with them.

"Now what do you think? Does he act like you're not his best friend?"

Scotty laughed, dodging another kiss from Buck. "See, he's happy to see you."

"Yep! Look Mommy, look how ph-b-uck loves me!"

"So the little runt found his way back." Chrissy waltzed into the room and sat next to Stetson. "I missed you. Naughty boy staying out all night."

"My daddy is not naughty!"

"Staying out all night with your ma is very very bad."

"Enough, Chrissy. I called Brian and he's coming to get you."

Chrissy smiled and flipped her long hair over her shoulder. "I know, he's already here. He went to town to arrange a few things."

Stetson and Storm exchanged uneasy glances.

The front door opened and in walked Brian. He looked good, tall, dark, and handsome. Stetson smiled at his friend. "Welcome, buddy."

Brian glared at Stetson, throwing him off balance.

"Did you get it all arranged?" Chrissy asked.

Brian frowned. Nodding he glared at Stetson. "All set for this afternoon. Who's this?" He nodded toward Storm.

"Just the baby mama. No one really." Chrissy stared at Storm with a smug smile.

Stetson was feeling more and more uneasy. "What's going on here?"

"You're going to marry your baby mama." Brian's stance made Stetson nervous. He'd seen Brian standoff with many cowboys over the years.

"What is going on?" Storm asked.

"Seems like old Stetson here has two baby mamas and this time he's marrying the second one. My sister!"

Stetson stood up. "Whoa. I don't know where you got your info, but it's a lie."

Brian's eyes grew dark. "You callin' my baby

sister a liar?"

"I never touched her."

"He did, Brian. It started before we left the rodeo circuit. That's why I followed him. It was heart breaking to find out about his little bastard and this slut."

Storm quickly picked Scotty up and took him upstairs.

"Out!" Stetson demanded taking a step closer to Brian.

"The wedding is all arranged." Brian took a step toward Stetson.

"Then unarrange it before I rearrange your face!"

"No can do. My sister will not be an unwed mother. Damn it Stetson, what were you thinking? I trusted you?"

Stetson could see the hurt and misery in Brian's eyes. "I swear-- Listen, lets go to see the doctor in the morning and then we can decide what to do."

Brian stepped back, rubbing the back of his neck. He almost looked relieved. "I can live with that."

"Well I can't," Chrissy shouted.

"Come on, Chris, let's go back to town, and find a place to stay."

"I have a place right here," she protested, her face turning red.

"Let me handle this," Brian said softly.

Chrissy stamped her foot. "They were out all night last night. I'm not leaving my Stetson with that barracuda again."

"She is the mother of my son. It might make you happy to know that she had no romantic inclinations toward me at all, but that does not excuse this whopper of a lie."

"Brian, he has to marry me today."

Brian gave Stetson a thoughtful look. Stetson could tell he was beginning to doubt his sister's claims.

"See you tomorrow," Brian said, dragging Chrissy behind him.

*****

Storm watched Buck and Scotty play in the yard. Trying to keep her mind off Chrissy's claim was near impossible. Five years ago, she would have instantly known Stetson was telling the truth. Now, she'd been through too much to trust. It made her sad to know she was still on her own, with Scotty.

Some lessons come hard, but they should not be forgotten. Trust no one and you can't be hurt. Sighing, she realized that her thinking was flawed. You could be hurt no matter what. It was better not to trust.

"Can I go on the next sleepover with you and Daddy?"

Storm looked up in surprise. "I don't think they'll be anymore sleepovers, kiddo."

Scotty's face scrunched up. "Daddy didn't put a snake in your sleeping bag did he?"

Laughing, she grabbed him up and kissed him all over his neck, making him squeal. "No, Daddy didn't put a snake in my sleeping bag."

"Only because I didn't think of it," Stetson said. He sat down in the grass next to them and lifted Scotty's shirt tickling him.

"Not fair, two against one!"

Stetson scooped Scotty up and whispered in his ear. Storm could tell by Scotty's smile that they were going to try to tickle her next. Pushing to her feet, she ran, but not fast enough. Suddenly she found herself on the ground with both Stetson and Scotty on top of her.

Trying to fight them off did no good. Stetson had her hands trapped above her head and he was kissing her neck. Scotty was tickling her underarms, making her scream for mercy.

They finally stopped, but Stetson still held on to her, his blue eyes boring into hers. The hunger in them blatant. There was also an expression that could be mistaken for tenderness, but Storm knew better. "Let go," she whispered, not taking her eyes from his.

He breathed hard and didn't move at first. He just kept staring. Suddenly he pushed off her and helped her up.

The giant step he took away from her hurt somehow. He was distancing himself from her.

"Come on, Mommy! Time to get Daddy!"

Storm gave them both a wistful smile. "I'm going to check on Nellie. You two have fun without me."

"Okay," Scotty shouted as he lunged himself at Stetson.

Her heart pinged. Scotty didn't seem to mind she was leaving. Stetson didn't seem to care either. She had to find somewhere else to live and fast. She didn't know how much longer she could take this estranged relationship with Stetson. It hurt too much.

*****

Storm wandered into the barn. The repairs were going really well. Scotty and Nellie were making cookies. Somehow, Nellie had talked Storm into staying for a while longer, claiming that with all the extra hands there was too much work to do. Nellie had a point. With all the workmen, new hands, and the arrival of new stock, Scott Ranch had become a hub of activity.

Scotty gloried in it. Stetson spent as much time with him as possible. More than Storm had ever expected. It had been a week and she hadn't heard a peep about Chrissy. Storm wasn't going to ask.

One thing that did bother her was the cause of the recline of the ranch. Somehow, it was all tied to her father. No one would give her a straight answer, which only piqued her interest more. She walked to Mitzi's stall, listening to her nicker. A nice ride across the land would calm her restless soul, but she didn't dare. She'd been getting too many looks from the new hands. Her reputation was well known and they all seemed to believe it.

The hope she would be free of such treatment shattered yesterday when a hand named Dickens tried to come on to her. He blocked her way out of the tack room and propositioned her. The lust in his eyes as they raked her body made her stomach turn. His shit-eatin' grin horrified her. Thankfully, Joe walked into the barn and Dickens walked away.

Her fear almost kept her from visiting her horse. She'd done nothing wrong; she had the right to hold her head up high, but Dickens had made her feel dirty.

She didn't dare tell Stetson. They were enjoying a bit of a truce these last few days and she didn't want to rock the boat. It shamed her that Dickens thought he had the right to treat her so. It seemed as soon as she got a bit of her self-confidence back, someone was always there to knock her back down.

Stroking Mitzi's neck, Storm wondered how long she'd be staying at the ranch. It was only a matter of time before she ended up causing trouble between the men. Stetson needed them to run the ranch. She was expendable, always. If only she could escape this town. If only she could start over again. Unfortunately, she needed money to do that.

She heard a truck drive up and went outside to see who it was. Stetson stood at the back of his truck grabbing packages, bags, and boxes. He turned toward her and smiled. "Come on, I bought you something."

Storm couldn't help the smile that crossed her face. Eagerly she followed him into the house.

Scotty stood on a chair covered in flour, waving a wooden spoon filled with batter around the kitchen, spraying it everywhere.

Nellie turned and laughed at the other two adults. "Don't worry, I know his parents and I'm sure they'll both want to clean up the mess."

"I think that's mommy duty." Stetson bravely walked toward the waving spoon and gently took it away. He hugged Scotty, both laughing when they realized that Stetson was now covered in flour.

Scotty spotted the bags and boxes. His eyes widened in wonder. "What's that? Groceries?"

Storm felt sad that Scotty was excited about groceries. That's what usually was in the bags she had brought home.

Nellie handed Scotty a damp cloth. "Wipe your hands and go see."

Scotty cleaned his hands in record time and jumped off the chair. He walked toward the packages, hesitantly.

Stetson grabbed a box and handed it to him. "Open it."

The little boy looked at his mother. Storm smiled and nodded. He opened the box and yelled, "Yahoo!" Grabbing a cowboy hat and a pair of boots, he ran to Storm. "Look!"

Storm's heart opened wide at Scotty's happiness. Stetson was a generous man. She accepted the bag he gave her. Looking in it, she saw jeans and t-shirts. She wanted to smile, but her bottom lip quavered instead. Her clothes were old and threadbare, but she always tried to do the best that she could.

Scotty was whooping again at the clothes he got. Tears filled her eyes. She wanted to feel grateful, but her heart felt judged. Once again, she wasn't good enough.

"Hey, cowboy, how about you and your Aunt Nellie get you cleaned up and then you can try on your cowboy gear."

Nellie nodded to him. Grabbing Scotty's new

clothes, she herded him up the stairs.

"Storm? Talk to me. I'm sorry, I shouldn't have just bought you clothes. I should have let you pick them out."

Turning, her eyes were filled with regret. "I'm sorry. Thank you. I needed new clothes. I haven't had anything new in about five years. Ever since my daddy put me off his ranch with only one suitcase, I've had to wear what I had."

Putting his hand on her soft cheek, he caressed it. "Tell me."

Giving him a sad smile, she shook her head. "It was hard enough to live through; I don't know if I can tell you. I blamed you for a lot of years."

"Not anymore?"

Her eyes sparkled with unshed tears. "I'm just less angry, more hurt. You never came back. I figured if you loved me like you said, you would have come back for me. But I guess that doesn't matter anymore. Thank you for the clothes."

Stetson took her into his arms. His palm cradled her head against his shoulder. He kissed her cheek and stared into her eyes He started to draw his lips down to hers when little feet running down the stairs interrupted the mood.

Stetson turned and grabbed up his son who had launched himself at him. "You look like a genuine cowpoke."

"Our hats are the same."

"We'll be the envy of cowboys everywhere."

"You can count me in as an envious cowboy," Joe said. "Nice duds."

"I'm not a dud."

Joe laughed, and then gave Nellie a big kiss. "Duds are cowboy clothes, Scotty. Yours are nice."

Scotty brightened. "My daddy boughted them. Now, let's go men, we have cattle to take care of."

Storm laughed. "All right, well you cowboys take care." She gave Stetson a mischievous look. "Nellie, what should we do all afternoon? No men around, we could paint our nails or something."

Stetson looked at Storm for help. "I really have a lot of work to do."

"I know, Daddy, let's go."

"Couldn't leave him?"

Storm smiled and shook her head.

"Okay, sport, let's go."

Stetson winked at Storm and left.

Later, Stetson looked tired. Storm had to hide her smile all throughout dinner. Scotty asked question after question about being a cowboy.

"Long day?"

Stetson nodded.

"Daddy, can we..." Scotty fell asleep mid sentence.

"Guess you tired him out." Storm stood to pick Scotty up.

Stetson got up and took Scotty from Storm. "Let's put him to bed."

Storm couldn't help but return his smile. Following him up the stairs, she was struck by how good he looked from the back. His shoulders were so brawny and wide, with lean hips. She blushed looking at his rear end. She had to admit, he was one sexy man. It was harder and harder to ignore that fact.

Moving in front of him, she pulled back the covers, while Stetson laid him down. Pulling off Scotty's shoes, Stetson pulled the covers up and kissed his cheek.

Talk about pulling at her heartstrings. He didn't want her though. No one wanted her in a loving, respectable way. She should be used to it, but it still hurt.

Stetson grabbed her hand, surprising her. "Let's go out for a walk."

She peered at him. "I thought you were tired."

"I am. I need to know what happened while I was gone. I need the details."

Storm gazed into his blue eyes wondering if it was a good idea to drudge everything back up. "It was an extremely painful time. I don't know if I can go through it again."

Stetson squeezed her hand, his eyes full of tender concern. Without answering him, she followed him outside.

They walked under the brightly lit Texas sky. The full moon seemed to glow just for them. Storm enjoyed the quiet companionship they shared. It was nice to be comfortable around him again.

Stetson gestured to a log lying in the grass. "Let's sit."

Storm tensed, but nodded. "I don't know where to begin."

"Why did your father make you leave?"

She could feel her throat tighten as she remembered. Her heart felt heavy. Maybe it would help to talk about it. "The day after you left, I went to talk to your father. I wanted to know where you went and when you'd be back. He went on and on about how you weren't coming back. I told him that I was pregnant and he laughed at me." She took a deep breath.

"I'm sorry."

"He said it wasn't yours and I'd better not tell anyone it was. He told me I'd be sorry if I did. I left broken hearted. I went home to my daddy. I told him everything. Oh, Stetson, he was livid. He went racing over to see your dad. When he got back, he gave me ten minutes to pack my things. He had Dugger drive down the long drive and leave me at the side of the road."

"Why didn't you tell me you were pregnant?"

Storm gazed at him, and smiled sadly. "I was going to tell you that night. Luck was not on my side. For a while, I wasn't even sure if God was on my side. I walked to town and I got a job at Daley's General Store. I even rented a room from them on the second floor. No one knew I was pregnant, and people were mad that my daddy threw me out."

"You're shivering." Stetson pulled her close, and put his arms around her. "I wish I'd never left. It kills me to think of what you've been through."

Storm nodded. "My daddy wasn't about to let the townspeople think badly of him, so he told the world that I was pregnant. I guess your father felt the need to tell one and all that I was a whore and it wasn't your baby." Tears filled her eyes. "It all went to hell after that. The Daley's fired and evicted me. I went everywhere looking for a job. No one would hire me. Only Miss Harriet and Miss Mable from the Tea and Yarn Shop were sympathetic, but they didn't have a job for me."

"I can hear the pain in your voice. We can do this another time." Stetson looked at her concerned.

"No, it's now or never. Frank from Faye's Diner finally gave me the waitressing job, graveyard shift. I found a place to live. I didn't know what was going to happen, but at least I had a roof over my head." She stood up and looked off into the distance. "When Scotty was born I had one visitor, your father. He wanted to be sure that I did not name my son Scott. He wasn't worthy of the Scott name."

"You named him after me anyway."

Looking over the land, she continued. "I had to have a cesarean and there was no one to care for me or Scotty. I had to walk home from the hospital. I did my best. The hospital bills kept sucking me down. I still owe them money."

Stetson stood and walked to her. He turned her toward him and held her tight.

She relished his strength. "Scotty never went without food or clothes or love. I did the best I could do, but I always felt as though I fell short. If it hadn't been for

Mrs. Burns and Nellie, well, I hate to think about it. Men started showing up at my doorstep thinking I was easy. I guess when your father denied that Scotty was yours, every man in town threw his hat in the ring, claiming it could be his."

Stetson pulled her closer and gently rocked her. He didn't say anything and Storm was glad. She didn't want to hear words of pity. Should she even take comfort from the man that left her? He could have called. He could have come back at anytime. He didn't.

Storm pulled away. "I can't do this with you. I'm still angry and very hurt. Where were you? I needed you but you left and never looked back!"

She expected denial, anger, anything would have been better than the tears she saw in his eyes. His heart was reaching out to hers; she could feel it and it astounded her. Storm tried to glance away, but he held her eyes with his. It wasn't pity or anger; it was sorrow and tender concern.

*****

Stetson grabbed her hand. He wasn't going to let her walk away. Listening to her, his heart tore in two. He knew that it had been difficult, hard even, but he really had no idea. Nellie had tried to tell him, but he never comprehended what it all meant. "You're right. I should have called. I should have come back. My pride got in the way. My fight with my father got in the way."

Gently wiping away a tear from her cheek with the pad of his thumb, he found it hard to breathe. "There was never one day that I didn't think of you. I was a fool to leave you and a bigger fool for not coming back for you. I was too busy trying to show my father that I was a winner."

Storm gave him a ghost of a smile. "You did that. The local paper carried all the news of your wins.

There was always a picture of you with a beautiful woman on your arm."

"And it hurt you." Stetson didn't wait for an answer. "I-- no one compared to you. I wasn't a saint, but it didn't take me long to realize that I left my heart behind when I left."

"I don't know if I can believe you. All I know is that we have a wonderful son and I do not want him hurt in any way."

"You know you're beautiful when your blue eyes flash like that?"

Storm shook her head. "I can't think about that or you."

Stetson nodded and pulled her close for another hug. "Just let yourself lean on me a little bit. That's all I want." She smelled of lilacs and he buried his face in her hair. Baby steps were what he'd have to take, but he was not a patient man. "I'm sorry for all the hurt my leaving caused. I'm sorry for all the heartbreak. I can't believe our fathers did all that damage to your reputation."

Storm snuggled against him. "That was one thing I could never figure out."

He felt as though they'd been robbed. They could have been married and who knew, maybe another child would have come from their union. What had he done that made his father hate him so? Storm was left behind to bear his wrath.

Her father had been just as bad. Why throw her out? The guilt he felt went soul deep. He should have stayed. He didn't know Storm was pregnant, but he should have stayed.

All his life, his dream had been to ride in the rodeo. He was good at it, damn good. Why couldn't his father have understood that? It wasn't going to be forever, but the old cuss gave him an ultimatum: stop riding in the rodeo or leave.

He remembered packing, putting his horses on

his trailer, and heading out to the McCrory ranch. Storm's father refused his request to see her. In fact, he told Stetson that Storm had always known he'd leave, that his love was untrue.

It had cut him so deep that he practically staggered to his truck. Then he left. Somehow, no matter how much he tried, he couldn't get Storm off his mind. There had been many groupies that wanted to be his, but no one measured up to Storm. That's why taking care of Chrissy came in handy. He told other women that he had to take care of his sister.

He never imagined the hell Storm had been through.

Kathleen Ball

CHAPTER EIGHT

Storm looked down at Scotty's eager face. He wanted them to go to town with Stetson. Storm didn't think it was a good idea. People had been cruel to her.

"Just to the store and that's it."

Scotty jumped up and down. He was wearing his cowboy hat and his boots. It was really incredible just how much he looked like his father. Storm said a silent prayer and walked out the door.

Scotty jumped into the truck and Storm was about to follow when she felt Stetson's hand on her giving her unneeded help. She didn't even look at him. Ever since their moon lit talk, he'd been finding all kinds of reasons to touch her. It was nice to be friends again though.

"I want to get candy and a new belt and a big bone for Buck and a present for Mommy and one for Aunt Nellie. Then I'm going--"

"Hold on champ. One thing at a time," Stetson said, smiling.

"Scotty, you know that Mommy doesn't have that much money. Maybe we could get a few things, but--"

"Daddy is rich and I can have anything I want!" Scotty crossed his arms and gave her a look of mutiny.

95

Storm felt her mouth drop open. When did her kind loving little boy turn into a spoiled child? "Turn around."

"What?" Stetson asked.

"We are going home. I will not have you buying things for my son. He never acted like this before."

Stetson ignored her and kept driving. Her anger grew with each turn of the truck's wheels. She wasn't going to fight in front of Scotty, but Stetson was going to get an earful.

Stetson parked the truck and Scotty scrambled out his side. She saw Stetson lean down and talk to Scotty. Joining them on the sidewalk, Storm wanted to scream at Stetson, but she held it in.

Scotty stood right in front of her and held out his arms. Storm picked him up. "I'm sorry, Mommy. I was just excited. Daddy said we will only get what you say."

His sorrow-filled eyes were her undoing. Hugging him tight, she kissed his cheek. "Let's go shopping." Putting Scotty down, she gave Stetson a look that she hoped said 'wait until I get you alone'.

Storm hated going into the general store. She always remembered how nice they had been, and then how callous they became. Evicting a pregnant woman was just so wrong. Holding her head up high, she followed Stetson and Scotty into the store.

Mrs. Daley gave Stetson a great big welcome home smile. Upon seeing Storm and Scotty, she visibly stiffened and a look of disapproval crossed her face.

Stetson nodded to her, picked up Scotty, and took Storm's hand. "Nice day. We have a bit of shopping to do."

"I only take cash from that one," Mrs. Daley said, automatically.

"However you want to handle it is fine," he answered, politely. Storm could see the tick of his jaw and knew he was annoyed.

"Let's get B-Buck his ph-one." Scotty took off for the pet section.

Storm smiled at Stetson, her anger gone. They followed close behind. Scotty picked out a bone that was bigger than he could carry. Storm voiced her doubts, but Scotty had a million reasons why Buck deserved it. Finally, she gave in.

They went off on a secret mission at one point and Storm knew that they were picking out something for her. It would be Scotty's first time buying her a present. She loved his homemade presents, but he seemed so excited and proud.

"Well, now we need to buy something for Scotty," Stetson announced.

Storm felt embarrassed. She had all of ten dollars on her. It wouldn't buy much. "Stetson, money is a bit tight, maybe some candy...." Looking away, she wanted to cry.

Scotty wrapped his arms around her legs. "It's okay, Mommy. I don't need anything."

A lone tear trailed down her face. Stetson kissed her cheek. "We'll worry about the money when we get home."

"She's got you wrapped around her little finger!"

Storm turned and was shocked to see Chrissy standing there with a tall, dark, cowboy named Evers. He had a mean streak a mile long. "I didn't realize you were still in town."

"From what I hear, you're pretty clueless about a lot of things." Chrissy stared at her.

"Hey, did you finally convince someone to be a daddy to your boy?" Evers asked, his voice dripping with sarcasm. He had been one of the men that thought he could knock on her door for a good time.

Stetson stepped in front of Storm and Scotty. "Chrissy, I heard you left. Where are you staying?"

"Storm's daddy took me in. He didn't think it

right that you got me in the family way and denied it."

Storm's gasp was loud. Her heart felt as though a knife was filleting it. Her father let Chrissy move in after he had thrown her out? Feeling sick to her stomach, Storm quickly rushed out of the store.

Leaning against the truck, she tried to breathe deep. What the hell? Why? Was she such an awful daughter? Why?

Soon enough, Stetson and Scotty came out with their purchases. Stetson helped her into the truck and gave her hand a quick squeeze. She tried to give him a semblance of a smile, but she failed.

*****

Stetson waited anxiously for Storm to yell at him all day. He knew she was still mad he refused to turn the truck around and go home. He also knew Chrissy and Evers upset her. She'd been pert near to crying on the way home.

It was after dinner and she still hadn't mentioned anything. It was starting to worry him. She had a delicate, lost look about her. It hurt to look at her. She sat by the fireplace and stared into it, although it was empty. What was she thinking? How could he comfort her?

"Like this, Daddy?" Scotty asked, as he fitted one Lincoln Log on another.

"Exactly. Boy, you sure are smart and a quick learner to boot. If I recollect correctly, it took me a few weeks to master the building of Lincoln Logs. You must get your smarts from your mommy."

Scotty smiled broadly. "Did you hear that, Mommy? Daddy says I'm smart!"

Storm smiled, the love she felt for her son beaming on her face. "You have a good daddy."

"You betcha!" Scotty got up and began to chase Buck. He had grabbed one of the logs and wanted to chew on it. "I got you the biggest bone ever and you still want my toys!"

Storm finally laughed and the haunted look left her face. "Time for bed, guys."

"Did you hear that, Daddy? Mommy said guys. That means more than one. It means you and me. Get it? You plus me is guys."

Stetson felt his laughter rumble through him. "Smart as a whip! I think your mommy meant you and Buck."

"Mommy?" Scotty stared at her with big eyes.

"Well, I really did mean you and Buck, but now that you mention it, maybe it is Stetson's bedtime."

"Saved by the bell," Stetson sighed in relief. A truck was driving toward the house. "Looks like ranch business."

"I can wait," Scotty said, earnestly.

Storm took his little hand. "Come on, kiddo, I'll read you a story."

Scotty looked sad. "Okay, if I have to."

After kissing his son's cheek, Stetson watched them go upstairs. His thoughts quickly changed to the men walking up to the front door. He recognized the tall, sandy haired, man as Garrett O'Neill, a fellow rancher. He wasn't familiar with the other man with black hair and eyes.

He opened the door and gestured for the men to come inside. "Garrett, good to see you."

They shook hands and Garrett turn toward the other man. "This is Stamos Walker. He owns a ranch in Lasso Springs too."

"Nice to meet you, Stamos. I know I've heard your name somewhere. You aren't the ex-FBI agent are you?"

Stamos shook Stetson's hand, smiling. "Guilty."

"Come on in to my office and you can let me know what I can do for you."

All three men walked into Stetson's rather

Kathleen Ball

cluttered office.

"Don't allow anyone in here to clean?" Garrett asked, his eyes blue twinkling in humor.

"How's Callie?"

Garrett's eyes lit up. "She's fine and dandy. She wants to get to know Storm."

Stetson nodded. "And you own the prison release ranch?" he asked Stamos.

"Yes I do. My wife Joy also wants to be a busybody and get to know your wife."

"We're not married."

"Well, that won't matter to Joy."

Tension melted from his body. Stetson didn't realize how much Storm's lack of friends disturbed him. "Good. So what's up?"

Stamos sat down on the black leather couch next to Garrett. "There have been a lot of cattle that have gone missing lately. I need to know how many head you've lost."

"I don't even know. My father left this place a shambles when he died. Something happened, I know we have missing cattle, but I'll be damned if I know any of the details."

Garrett and Stamos exchanged looks. "That's what we figured," Garrett said. "The only problem is that all trails lead to this ranch."

Stetson felt the breath whoosh out of him. "What are you implying?" His voice was cold as stone.

"That's why I had Garrett come with me. I need you to trust me. I know you've been set up. I just don't know how or by who," Stamos told him.

"The who is easy. Have you talked to McCrory?" Stetson asked.

Garrett laughed. "Funny, he told us to talk to you. Seriously though, we think it's McCrory too. We just haven't been able to get any evidence."

"What about the local authorities?" Stetson asked.

Stamos shook his head. "They aren't interested in helping. We're investigating on our own and we'd like you to join us."

Stetson looked from one man to the other. "What do you need me to do?"

"Well, for starters, we need to get our women together in town so that our being seen around together doesn't tip off anyone. They'll just think we're all just friends," Garrett explained.

"Then?" Stetson asked, rubbing his hand over his whiskered face.

"Then we compare notes and figure this whole mess out," Stamos said.

*****

Storm wanted to run and hide. Stetson and Nellie wanted them all to go to church. Her heart leapt out of her chest at the thought of the whole town looking at her. Disappointment washed through her. She'd thought Stetson understood how much it hurt her to go into town. Gazing at Nellie and Stetson seated at the kitchen table, she felt betrayed. They didn't understand her. They didn't have her back.

Nellie's blue eyes appeared hopeful, making it hard to say no. Plastering on a fake smile, Storm simply nodded.

The smile Nellie bestowed on her should have reassured her. It usually did, but not this time.

Breakfast no longer held its appeal. Her stomach churned. No matter how hard she tried to concentrate on Scotty, her mind whirled. She remembered every insult, every slight. Why would they expect her to go? For Scotty's sake, she supposed.

"You go on and get ready, I'll take care of the munchkin," Stetson told her. He was already wiping Scotty's face. "I'll get him dressed. Go on."

She could feel the heat of his intense perusal. Shoving her chair back, she got up to go. Shaking her head, she wanted to say no. She wanted to tell them that they were all crazy. If it had just been Stetson she would have, but she couldn't disappoint Nellie.

One dress graced her closet. Stetson had bought it for her and she didn't want to wear it. Fear stopped her in her tracks. She was going to charge down those stairs and just tell them to forget it. She was a grown woman and she could make her own decisions! Grabbing the door handle, she stopped, realizing that Stetson would just take Scotty with him anyway. There was no way she was going to allow Scotty to be subjected to all those stares without her.

"Almost ready?" Nellie called through the door.

Patience, Storm closed her eyes and prayed for patience. "Almost."

"Meet you downstairs. We have to leave in about five minutes."

The blue dress beckoned to her from the closet. Hastily she put it on. It was a good fit and it was actually pretty. She thought that the sleeveless dress with its V-neck and fitted waist, made her shape look a lot better than it really was. Picking up the white short jacket, she left the room.

Thank God for Nellie. The whole ride there, Scotty wanted to know about God and God's house. Storm didn't feel up to answering his questions. Nellie, Joe, and Scotty sat in the back while she sat in the front next to Stetson.

Glancing at his handsome face didn't give her an inkling what he was thinking. He must realize it might get nasty. He certainly didn't look worried.

A feeling of dread engulfed her as she stepped out of the car. Scotty chattered happily in Stetson's arms. Biting her bottom lip, she walked toward the white church. Stetson caught up and took her hand. It startled her, and it puzzled her.

His eyes bore into hers. He smiled at her, his cute dimples showing. "We'll be fine. Remember, I'm here."

Storm felt a bit of relief when he entwined his fingers with hers. It felt strangely intimate. Nodding, she took a deep breath and allowed Stetson to lead them in.

Any slight hope, she'd had that maybe it would be all right faded as soon as they crossed the threshold. First, there was hushed silence, then mouth dropping stares, and finally the whispering behind hands. Staring straight ahead, trying to ignore them, didn't work.

Stetson leaned down and whispered in her ear. "Chin up, you've done nothing wrong."

Once again, Storm felt her fake smile plaster her face. She'd smile if it killed her. She'd do it for Scotty's sake. Stetson kissed Scotty on the cheek and Storm finally became aware of what the whole going to church thing was about. Stetson was claiming Scotty as his son. He was letting the whole town know.

A seed of hope planted itself in her heart. She could do this. She'd put up with it for years now. She could do this for her son. Maybe now Scotty would be accepted. She didn't care about herself, but she did care what others thought of her son.

Walking up the aisle to a pew near the front, Stetson squeezed her hand. Looking at him, he smiled again. This time her smile wasn't fake. Stetson was trying to help.

Storm watched as he let go of her hand and shook the hands of two men in the pew behind them. One she recognized as Garrett O'Neill, though she hadn't seen him in years. The dark haired man she didn't know.

Garrett smiled at her. He was still a handsome devil with his blue eyes and broad shoulders. "Storm, good to see you. This is my wife, Callie. You might remember her from high school."

Callie smiled at her. "Hi Storm. Long time, you

look great."

Storm stared at the blond blue-eyed beauty and smiled. "Thanks." The lump in her throat was too large for her to say anything more.

Callie turned toward the woman beside her. "This is Joy and her husband Stamos."

Stamos nodded politely while Joy grabbed her hand. "Been waiting to meet you. Let's get together soon."

The friendship they offered blew Storm away. Callie and Garrett looked happy with their toddlers. One, a beautiful little girl, and the other cherub, a handsome boy.

Joy and Stamos were busy trying to quiet a little boy about two years of age that looked just like Stamos with his jet-black hair and beautiful brown eyes. Joy held a baby in her arms. A little girl if the color of the blanket was an indication. Her dainty features were adorable.

Gazing at Stetson, Storm felt safe. It had been so lonely for her. Her heart squeezed with how these people were willing to be her friends.

They gathered outside the church after the service. Storm felt blessed. There were still stares and whispers, but Storm felt stronger. Stetson's concern for her allowed her to hold her head up high.

Observing the circle of friends she suddenly had, she relaxed. She didn't know how or why, but gratefulness filled her heart. Her body was singing from sitting next to Stetson all morning. It seemed as though he took every opportunity to brush against her, leaving her tingling all over.

Desire she had thought long buried, filled her being. Her thoughts were on his full lips. What would it be like to kiss again?

Stetson gave her a knowing smile. He'd caught her staring. Her face began to heat and she just knew a telling blush was surfacing. Quickly she looked away from his sexy grin only to find everyone staring at her.

"Storm is that okay with you?" Joy asked, her

long brown hair blowing in the wind. Joy handed her baby to Stamos and gathered her hair, braiding it. "I think we ladies deserve some alone time."

Joe leaned down and kissed Nellie's cheek. "Well, I'll head home. Call when you need a ride."

Nellie's blue eyes grew wide. "You are not going anywhere. You are going to the park with the rest of the dads. You need the practice."

A tremendous hush stole over the crowded parking lot. Everyone turned and gawked at Nellie. "I hadn't planned to announce it quite like that." Tears filled her eyes.

Joe pulled her into his strong arms, rubbing his hands up and down her back. "It's all right, sweetheart." Then in a loud voice he announced their engagement.

Tension filled Storm's body. She knew just how cruel people could be. Remembering her disgrace filled her with shame. Quickly she took Nellie's hand and offered her congratulations. It warmed her heart to see others follow in kind.

Stetson came to stand at her side, putting his arm around her shoulder. Leaning down, he kissed her temple and whispered his thanks to her. The tingling began again. She wasn't sure what was worse, tension or tingling.

"Okay, enough," Callie announced. "Come on gals, let's go have some coffee."

"Coffee?" Storm asked.

Callie laughed. "You can't keep that man on your mind twenty-four/seven. We planned to go to the diner and have the men take the kids to the park."

Panic seized her. "I can't go to the diner. I, I--" She turned toward Stetson for help.

"If you mean because of Bailey, don't you worry none," Callie told her, her violet eyes were filled with concern.

"We have it on good authority that Frank no

longer believes that you would steal from him. Besides, Bailey is not our favorite person," Joy told her.

"I don't understand."

Callie laughed. "That viper has tried to steal all of our men at one time or another. Come on, let's go for coffee."

Storm didn't know what to think or feel. All kinds of emotions bombarded her.

Stetson nodded in encouragement. "Scotty, give Mommy a hug. We're going to the park."

"Oh boy!" Scotty gave Storm the briefest of hugs and began to pull Stetson by the hand toward the park.

Watching the men truck across the parking lot with babies, diaper bags, and strollers made them laugh. "Hope they can handle it," Callie muttered.

Joy put her arm around Nellie. "Joe will learn what not to do."

"That's for sure," Callie said, as they walked down the sidewalk of Lasso Springs. "Storm, you look like you're going to an execution. It'll be fine, I promise."

Giving Callie a brief smile, Storm followed them inside. It was crowded with all the people from church. It had never been this crowded during her graveyard shift. They followed Joy to a corner booth and sat.

Joy's cell phone rang. "I leave you for one minute and you call," she said into the phone. "In the diaper bags. Yes, just look." Joy shook her head exasperated, but her love for Stamos was evident.

"Let me guess," Callie said, when Joy got off the phone. "Diaper change?"

"No, he needed a bottle for Liberty. You know he raised Dillon for a few months without help. I just don't get men."

Storm smiled. She liked her new friends. She noticed a few stares, but she also noticed both Callie and Joy staring right back. "Don't lose friends on my account."

"I wouldn't worry about it, Storm," Callie told her. "Besides I'm having fun."

Callie's bright smile was infectious. Storm felt certain gladness. Slowly she relaxed and enjoyed the women's company.

"I don't think you're allowed in here," Bailey said, approaching their table. "Three coffees?" she asked, ignoring Storm.

"Yes three regular and one decaf," Callie told her.

"I'm not serving her." Bailey's normally pretty face turned ugly.

"Go ask Uncle Frank if you want to," Joy said, smugly.

Bailey huffed, spun on her heel, and stomped off.

"Uncle Frank?" Storm asked.

Joy laughed. "Well, maybe I stretched the truth. He's the uncle of one of our hands. Close enough."

"Oh boy. Here she comes," Nellie said, eagerly.

They were enjoying themselves, Storm realized. It was more than fine with her. Besides Stetson and Nellie, she'd stood alone for a long time.

Bailey's smile looked forced. "Here is your coffee ladies," she ground out, staring at Storm. "What else can I get you?"

"Why don't you bring us a piece of that peach pie my Aunt Elma makes," Joy told her.

"Aunt?" Callie asked, watching Bailey leave.

"She's Frank's wife," Joy told her, her blue eyes twinkling.

They all laughed. Storm's soul didn't feel as tattered.

*****

The dinner dishes were done, and Scotty was

tucked into bed. He'd had a great day at the park. Stetson smiled, thinking what a leader Scotty turned out to be. He had all the other kids following him around.

The screen door opened, and out came Storm with two steaming mugs in her hands. She handed one to Stetson before she sat next to him on the porch swing.

"Thanks for the coffee." Taking a sip, he gazed out into the night. "Long day, huh?"

Storm nodded. "Long but good. Your friends are nice."

"They're your friends now too."

Storm smiled at him. "It's nice to have friends again."

Stetson watched her sip her coffee. Her blond hair, pulled back into a ponytail, showed the gracefulness of her neck and her flawless skin. She looked more like a teenager than a mother.

"So tell me again. Whose kids are whose?"

Stetson sat back against the cushion. "Callie and Garrett have the twins, Aiden and Rose. Joy and Stamos have little Dillon and baby Liberty."

"They all seem to love their families very much."

Stetson detected the wistfulness in her voice. "Nicest people I know. They took a shine to you."

Storm's face grew red. "Think so?"

Nodding, Stetson put his arm around her shoulders. "I know so."

Storm glanced at him and then quickly looked away. He wondered what she saw when she looked at him.

"It was nice to have Joy and Callie defend me. I glowed when they put Bailey in her place, but now I feel bad."

"Bad?"

Storm nodded. "I know what it's like to have people humiliate you. I'm not saying she didn't deserve it, but I didn't take as much delight in it as I thought I might. But my heart feels lighter."

Stetson took her hand in his. He stoked the back of her hand with his thumb. "Lighter?"

Storm looked at him with twinkling eyes. "Some of the bitterness I've held in my heart toward Bailey is gone."

Leaning in, he gave her a quick kiss on her ripe lips. The look on her face was one of surprise. Storm put her fingers to her lips. He could see her trying not to smile, but she lost the battle.

"You are so beautiful, and too kind hearted for your own good." The look of pleasure she displayed warmed his heart. He felt as though they were growing closer. He wanted them to be a family, but it had to be Storm's choice.

"This is nice." Storm put her head on his shoulder. "Who's that?" Storm asked, spotting a car racing up the drive.

"Maybe you should go inside. Could be trouble."

"I'm not leaving. Oh hell, it's my father's car. Just run him off. Do you want me to get a rifle?"

Stetson looked at her earnest face and laughed. "I'm hoping we won't need it."

"But--"

The car door slammed, twice. Pat McCrory and Chrissy came around the front, heading toward them. Stetson was surprised to see them. McCrory's face appeared red while Chrissy's seemed smug.

"I take it this isn't a social visit." Stetson stared at McCrory.

"I'm just bringing your fiancé back to you."

Stetson's eyebrows rose. What was McCrory's game now? "Don't do me any favors."

McCrory took a step toward the porch steps. Stetson countered by standing at the top of the stairs.

"You got this little filly in the family way. There is only one way to fix this situation."

Storm gasped. "Why? You didn't care what

happened to me!"

Glancing over his shoulder Stetson saw the pain on Storm's face. It had to be a hard blow to her.

"Good to see you again, Chrissy. I heard you were still in these parts." Stetson nodded politely.

Chrissy took a step forward, standing beside, McCrory. "It's a good thing I didn't leave. Your baby needs a daddy."

Stetson wanted to laugh at her look of triumph. He didn't believe she was even pregnant and he knew for damned sure it wasn't his. "I never fornicated with you."

Chrissy gasped and McCrory tried to charge up the stairs. Stetson stood firm, his legs spread the width of his shoulders and his arms crossed in front of him. He'd fight if he had to; he hoped it wouldn't come to that. McCrory would just end up hurt and nothing would be solved.

"For your information, we made love," Chrissy screeched.

Stetson shook his head and stared at her. "No, honey, there is only one woman that I've ever made love with and that's Storm. I have to admit I wasn't any type of saint while I was on the road, but I never nailed you."

Chrissy grabbed McCrory's arms. "Do something. He's making it sound so dirty."

Stetson spotted the look of doubt on McCrory's face. "If you need help with the real daddy, let me know. I owe it to your brother. Anything else, I'm sorry you're out of luck."

He felt Storm step right behind him, she put her hand on his back, a show of support he imagined. It felt good to know that she believed in him.

McCrory took Chrissy by the arm and led her back to his truck. "You ain't seen the last of me."

Storm's body shook as she watched her father and Chrissy drive away. She put her hands over her mouth.

"It's going to be all right."

Storm, lowered her hand and a sob escaped. "Why? Why would he seek justice for Chrissy?" She turned away from Stetson. "He put me at the curb like yesterday's garbage."

"Storm look at me."

She shook her head. "I can't. I've gone over that day so many times in my head. You were gone, your father denied my baby was yours, and my father threw me out. Now he has the gall to show up looking to make you marry Chrissy? I was a good daughter. I really was, and I made one mistake, well no not a mistake. I got into a bad situation, and he turned his back on me."

"He never said why? No one has given you any clues?"

"All I know is that he went to see your father and when he came back, he told me to leave."

"How did he react to the news of your pregnancy?"

"At first he turned white, and had to sit down. He was mad at you. Then he suddenly left." She glanced over her shoulder. Turning, she walked until she stood right in front of Stetson. "You seem angry."

Stetson studied her face. Reaching out, he tucked a piece of her hair behind her ear. "He hurt you, of course I'm angry. He's still hurting you."

Swallowing hard she nodded. "Do you suppose your father said something to make him disown me?"

Stetson pulled her toward him. "We'll find the answers Storm. You need to know, I can see how it's eating at you. I don't know what happened, and I don't understand the whole Chrissy thing unless he was trying to get at me."

"A lot has happened in five years." Storm sighed against him.

"So it seems." Stetson placed a kiss on her temple.

"I did wonder one thing, Stetson. What happened to

your ranch? I never heard one word of its decline."

CHAPTER NINE

Storm's anxiety knew no bounds as she bounced around in Stetson's truck. The road to Stamos and Joy's ranch was beyond bumpy. The ride had been filled with an uncomfortable silence.

Stetson frowned. It had been his idea to hire Stamos to find out what happened between their fathers. He hadn't glanced in her direction even once.

Sighing, she wondered what they'd find out. Stetson had told her this morning her father was the reason the Scott ranch was almost bankrupt. Nothing made sense anymore. No one seemed to have any details as to what went wrong between the two men. There was no way she could ask her father. Hopefully, Stamos could help. Stetson said Stamos used to be FBI.

Storm smiled. The Walker ranch was a hub of activity. The whitewashed buildings looked new and well cared for, and there were horses everywhere. In the distance, she could see a good amount of cattle. Things appeared to be going well for her friends.

Getting out of the truck, they headed toward the house. An older woman was leading a grey horse out of the house. Storm looked at Stetson, but he didn't seem surprised.

"How many times do I have to tell you no kitchen?" the woman admonished the horse. Seeing them, she smiled and waved. "Go on in, Nanny and I have to have a little chat."

"What in the world?" Storm just couldn't believe it.

"That's Nanny. Don't tell me you haven't heard of Nanny?" Stetson smiled. "She belongs to Garrett and she roams. They call her the Houdini of horses; she goes from ranch to ranch, lets herself into the barn, greets her friends, and finds a stall for the night."

"You're teasing me. I don't believe you."

"True story. She has a daughter named Nino, a husband named Pirate, and a goat friend named Billy."

The door to the house opened and Joy stepped out. "Nanny?"

"Seems so." Stetson grinned and looked at Storm.

"I keep telling her, the porch is fine, but no kitchen." Joy shook her head. "Poor Bea hates it when this happens. Well come in, it's nice to see you."

"Good to see you too, Joy," Stetson said politely.

"Your ranch is lovely." Storm told her.

"Thank you. I think so too." Joy led them into the house.

"Might as well head on into the den. I have a feeling the kitchen isn't fit for company." She ushered them into a big room with a massive desk and dark leather furniture.

"We need to talk to Stamos," Stetson told her. He took off his hat and ran his fingers through his blond curls.

"He should be back any minute. He went to tend the horses with Dillon." Cocking her head, she smiled. "I hear my darling Liberty. I'll be back."

Storm felt amazed. "Did you notice that having a

horse in her house didn't even faze her?"

Stetson took her hand and pulled down onto the leather couch with him. "Can't wait to tell Scotty."

Storm smiled at him. He was so handsome. She just loved his beard and mustache. She loved the way it tickled when they kissed. She suddenly stopped smiling and turned away. What was she thinking? The feeling of desire didn't immediately leave her. Glancing at him, he gave her a roughish grin. "Stop smiling at me."

Stetson laughed.

"Joy says you want to see me?" Stamos asked, walking into the room. He immediately shook Stetson's hand and he nodded to her.

Stetson put his hand over Storm's. She was wringing them madly "I was hoping you'd be able to help us."

Stamos sat on a big leather chair across from them. "I'll do what I can. What do you need?"

"We need you to find out why my father is a nasty human being," Storm blurted. She peeked at Stamos and turned red. "Sorry. Stetson, you explain it."

Stetson squeezed her hands. "Our fathers started feuding when I left town and Storm revealed she was pregnant."

"Sounds like a good enough reason to me," Stamos said.

"After I left town, Storm told her father about the baby. McCrory raced over to see my dad and something must have happened or been said because he returned home, and threw Storm out. She was homeless."

Stamos looked sympathetic. "Sorry," he told Storm.

"I know you saw the condition of my ranch. I've been through all of my father's paperwork and I can't figure out where all his assets went. Rumor has it, McCrory had a hand in it."

"I think you're right Stetson. McCrory had something to do with all the cattle coming up missing in these parts. I've been looking into that. Maybe if I knew the reason, I'd know the how."

Joy entered the room, Liberty in her arms. "Well, Nanny didn't do too much damage. Dillon is helping Bea make cookies. I think Dillon is making a bigger mess than Nanny ever did." She examined them one by one. "Did I interrupt something? You all look so grim."

Stamos stood up and went to his wife and daughter. He kissed Joy on the cheek and put his finger in front of Liberty for her to take hold. "She's a strong one."

"She's beautiful." Storm heard the wistfulness in her voice. They'd been robbed.

"I think we're done, aren't we?" Storm asked.

"I got enough to go on. I'll call later."

Stetson shook Stamos' hand. "We appreciate it."

*****

They weren't on the road long. Storm tried to avoid glancing at Stetson. It seemed old wounds kept opening and it was taking a toll on her. Staring out the window, Storm smiled when she saw the Queen Anne's Lace swaying in the wind. Was she ever so carefree that she ran through the fields picking the white flowers? It was hard to remember.

"Storm, are you all right?" Stetson's eyes were full of concern. Too much concern. A lump formed in her throat and she found it hard to talk.

She gave him a quick nod, and turned toward the window again. She wasn't sure she even wanted to know why her father threw her out. She already knew she'd failed him by getting pregnant.

Stetson covered her hand with his. She hadn't realized how cold her hands were until his warm one encountered hers. Looking down, she could see the contrast in size and strength. Stetson was always the strong one.

She'd become pretty strong herself in recent years she conceded. "Do you think Stamos will come up with anything?"

Stetson squeezed her hand gently. It felt so reassuring. "I don't know if he'll be able to find out the why, but I have confidence he'll find out the how. There has to be some record of where all the livestock went."

"Maybe I could go back and see my father. I could look around."

The truck lurched as Stetson slammed on the brakes. "No way in hell are you going over there!"

He was probably right, but ultimatums did not sit well with her. "Stetson, I know you think you can tell me what to do, but surprise-- you can't."

Stetson stared at her. The expression of disbelief on his face almost made her laugh. People probably didn't disobey him very much. He continued to stare and a variety of emotions crossed his face. His handsome face. The deep sorrow and concern almost made her cry. The concern suddenly turned to desire. She could see it in his eyes.

The tension in the cab of the truck grew thick, as her heart began to beat wildly. Desire washed over her. She wanted, she needed his lips on hers, his hands on her body. He leaned toward her, and to her amazement, she met him half way.

He cradled her cheek in his big palm and kissed her. He kissed her long and hard, meeting her tongue with his.

His lips were magic, his kiss made her squirm with desire. Running her fingers through his blond curls, she felt alive. She belonged in his arms. He pulled her closer, and she willingly went.

Stetson kissed her neck, she shivered. He put his hands up her tee shirt and covered her breasts. Moaning, she pressed herself against him. She wanted him to take off her bra, and her wish instantly came true.

Butterflies swarmed her stomach when he removed her shirt

"Take off your shirt, Stetson. I want to feel your bare chest against mine." Storm helped with the buttons until his bare chest was exposed. She gasped. He was all muscle with a sprinkling of blond hair. How delicious.

Stetson groaned as her hands explored his chest, and moved downward. His eyes widened as she unbuttoned his jeans. "You're trying to kill me."

Storm smiled at him. "Shuck those pants, cowboy."

Stetson laughed. "You first."

Storm looked into his eyes. They were pooled with desire. She wanted him with a fierceness that scared her. Hurriedly, she took off her jeans and panties and was delighted to see Stetson doing the same. "Oh."

"What? You've seen it before."

"Yes, but well, I guess my memory didn't do you justice."

Quickly, he reached for her, and sat her on top of him. Storm gasped. It felt so good. It felt absolutely, sinfully, wonderful.

Leaning forward she kissed his neck, her nails driving into his shoulders. The feel of his mouth on her sent her over the edge and she cried out. The intensity of it awed her. She continued stroking his beard and kissing his neck.

Stetson shuddered and held her close. "Oh God!"

Storm nodded her head against him. "Yes, Oh God is right. Did it used to be that good?"

Stetson's laugh rumbled through his body making her shiver. "You don't remember?"

Storm grew serious and she sat back from him so she could read his face. "I remember every single time we were together. I remember the way you touched me, I remember how good you smelled, and I remember that I felt loved in your arms. I've thought about it plenty through the years."

"Oh, sweetheart, I remember too. I knew the entire time I was gone that it was a mistake and you were the only one for me. I just had too much pride to come back to see my father."

Storm leaned in for a long slow kiss. She'd be mad at herself later. Right now, it felt too good, and she wanted to grab and hold on to the happiness of the moment.

"We steamed up the windows," Stetson said, as they heard a horn honk.

"Oh hell, where are my clothes?" Storm scrambled around the seat until she found all of them. Quickly she dressed, throwing Stetson's clothes at him.

"It's fine."

She shook her head. "No. It's not fine. People will talk. I made a mistake." Her eyes glistened. "Please take me home."

Stetson gave her a long probing look. Finally, he nodded and started the truck. Neither spoke on the way home.

*****

Driving up toward his house, Stetson decided that no matter what he wasn't sorry about making love with Storm. He could understand her misgivings, but he knew what happened. He knew how good it was and he knew she enjoyed it.

Sighing, he contemplated her. She hadn't glanced in his direction the whole ride home. Well, he'd let her brood for a while, then they were going to talk. There had to be a way to erase all her doubts.

"What in the world?" Storm asked, spotting Scotty running from the house. His face was all splotched as if he'd been crying.

Stetson stopped the truck and they immediately got out. Stetson reached his despondent son, first. Picking him up he could feel the sobs rack Scotty's whole body.

Storm was quickly at his side, rubbing Scotty's back and speaking softly to him. "What's wrong, baby?"

"You ticked Daddy and he's not my daddy!" His wailing grew louder.

Nellie was immediately by their side. "Let's take him inside. We went to town and he overheard some nasty gossip."

Alarm and panic set on Storm's face. They all knew she'd been dreading that this would happen.

"It's going to be okay." He hoped to hell that he was right.

Buck raced toward them. He was distressed to see Scotty so upset. He barked and barked. Storm leaned down and scooped him up. He strained out of her arms to be with Stetson and Scotty.

"Here, I can carry both." Stetson stopped and gathered up the puppy. Buck immediately whined at Scotty then licked his face. He whined again and looked depressed.

Stetson plopped them all down on the couch. "Scotty, tell me what happened."

The sadness on his son's face made his heart twist. He realized that when your child hurt, you hurt.

Storm handed Scotty a tissue and had Scotty blow his nose. "Kiddo, tell me what you heard. I'm sure it was some mistake."

Scotty nodded. "The lady said I was a mistake."

Storm gasped and her gaze flew to Stetson's. "Of course that's not true."

Scotty nodded. "That's what Aunt Nellie said. She said that God doesn't make mis-- misss-takes."

Stetson kissed Scotty's head and held him closer on his lap. "Your Aunt Nellie is right."

Scotty turned his big eyes toward Storm. "She

saided that you ticked Daddy. Daddy is not my real daddy. I want him to be my real daddy. Mommy, why did you tick him?"

Storm appeared confused, then angry. "Where did you take him?"

Joe walked in with a pot of coffee and three mugs. "We went into the pizza place. We met up with Lola and her daughter Meggie. Meggie wanted to play a song on the jukebox and Scotty went with her. Nellie's not to blame."

Storm walked over and hugged Nellie. "I didn't mean to blame you. I'm sorry."

"I feel so bad." Nellie's eyes filled.

"No more crying. I have two mugs of my special hot chocolate for two special people," Joe told them.

"Oh boy." Scotty jumped off Stetson's lap and followed Joe.

"Hot chocolate trumps all. I'll have to remember that." Stetson grabbed Storm's hand and pulled her down beside him. She snuggled close to him. It made him feel ten feet high that she was seeking comfort from him.

"Who?" Storm asked.

Nellie shook her head. "Scotty never said a word until we were on our way home. Then he started crying. It took a while to figure out what had happened. I tried everything, but he was heartbroken."

"It was bound to happen, I suppose." Stetson smiled watching Scotty carefully carry his mug over to them. Buck was right behind him carrying a big bone.

"Look at Unka Joe boughted Buck!"

"That's a really big bone." Storm told him, taking his mug, and setting it on the table.

"Uh huh and look!" Scotty stretched out the front of his blue shirt. "High Ho Silver, away." He repeated himself, skipping around the room pretending to be riding a horse.

"That's great, son."

Scotty stopped and looked at Stetson. "Are you my real daddy?"

The doubt and hope in Scotty's eyes almost made Stetson break down. "Yes I am. I'm your daddy. Heck don't we look alike?"

Scotty smiled and nodded. "Mommy, did you tick Daddy?"

Storm held her arms open and Scotty went flying into them. "Of course not. I wouldn't do that."

"Good! Are we getting married?"

Storm looked stunned. Scotty put his hand on her face until she was looking right at him. "Mommies and daddies get married. Everyone knows that. I want to marry Daddy." He nodded his head and smiled, as if it was a done deal.

"It's a fine idea." Stetson smiled at Storm. She didn't smile back. In fact, she looked horrified. "What? It wouldn't be so bad."

Storm looked at him again. "We'll talk about it later."

"Uh oh, Daddy. That means no."

"Really?"

"Yes, Daddy I know about these things. I knowed Mommy a long time." His eyes were wide and serious. At least he'd stopped crying.

"Well, bud, you and I are going to have to think of a way to make her say yes."

"Oh boy!"

"Whoa. I'm not sure..."

Scotty touched her cheek again, making her look at him. "It's my job to make you say yes."

Storm smiled and shook her head. "I don't know about you two. It's naptime for three of you."

"Ha ha. You, me, and Daddy."

Storm laughed. "No, you, Buck, and Aunt Nellie"

"Come on Daddy, you can tuck me and Buck in.

He can't bring his bone on my bed. He did that last time and he slobbered and you know what?"

Stetson picked up both Scotty and Buck. Scotty chattered to him all the way up the stairs.

Kathleen Ball

CHAPTER TEN

Storm stopped Mitzi by the fence line. The fence separated her father's land from Stetson's. Patting the freckled Appaloosa on the neck, she took in the sight of the land she had ridden over almost every day since she could sit a saddle. A wave of sadness blew over her, like the cool Texas wind. It made her shiver. Nothing made sense.

The hurt and humiliation she suffered at the hands of her father kept her from examining the whole situation. She never did get a reason for his callousness. Now, she didn't know what to think.

It was still so clear in her mind. She'd tearfully told her father that she was pregnant. He had hugged her, and told her everything was going to be all right. He kissed her forehead and left. He went to see Stetson's father. When he came back, he was enraged, and ordered her to leave. What had Mr. Scott said to her father? Why did he believe him without not so much as a word to her?

Taking off her riding glove, she wiped away a lone tear. It was hard to move on when the past still had such a hold on her. In the distance, she saw a lone rider. She'd know him anywhere. Her father still sat in a saddle straight and tall.

He stopped his horse, and gazed at her. He couldn't see her features as they were too far away. His stare seemed to last forever, before he turned and rode away.

Storm swallowed hard, put her glove back on, and pointed Mitzi toward home. If everyone had their way, it would be her home permanently. The last few days had exhausted her.

Scotty expected to be best man, and was adamantly backed up by Stetson. Nellie wanted to know if she had a dress in mind. Joe wanted to know if they reserved the church yet. It went on and on.

No one wanted to listen to her objections, her concerns. To all of them including the insufferable Stetson, it was a done deal. He walked around with a shit-eating grin on his face and God help her she felt compelled to wipe it off.

He'd left before. He could just as easily leave again. Men weren't permanent. They couldn't be counted on. She needed to make her own way in the world. She would never again be at the mercy of a man's whim or anger. The problem was what to do. How would she make her way? She wanted to go back to school and take computer classes. She wanted to create websites for ranchers. She'd already read up on most of the technology and she found there was a need for such sites.

Shrugging, she pushed on home. Castles in the air. She remembered hearing the term somewhere, and it fit. Dreams led to disappointment, she knew that. It had been a lesson hard learned. She felt like jumping out of her skin and running. If not for Scotty, she would. She'd run far away where no one knew her.

All dreams again. She'd have to stop if she wanted to hold on to her sanity. Stetson didn't love her. He just wanted Scotty. He denied it, but she knew in her heart it was the truth. If he had loved her, he would have come back long ago. Now that was the truth.

Riding into the yard, Storm was amazed to see Scotty and Stetson standing before a motley crew of animals. Getting closer, Mitzi shook her head in greeting. "Oh my."

Scotty ran to her side as she climbed out of the saddle. "Mommy, we have company."

His face glowed with excitement and she admitted to herself that living at the ranch had been good for him. "We do? Where?"

"Oh, Mommy, you are silly. Right there." He waved his hand toward the animals.

The animals seemed to line themselves up by height. A large black stallion stood at the beginning, then Nanny the grey horse, followed by another, younger grey, a goat, and then Buck. A very bizarre sight.

Stetson took her hand and gently tugged her forward. "Come meet our company."

Storm smiled at the teasing glint in his eyes. "What on earth?"

"Mommy, let me introduce you. This is Pirate, he's Nanny's husband. They are *married.*" Scotty stared at her.

Storm pretended she didn't get his meaning. "Who is next?"

"That's Nino, she's Pirate and Nanny's little girl. They are *married.*" Scotty gave her another owlish stare.

Storm quickly looked at Stetson and almost laughed watching him trying not to smile. No help there. "And the goat?"

"That's Billy," he paused and looked at her again. "Get it, Billy goat? And guess what, he's a she."

She couldn't help herself, she finally laughed. Leaning over, she picked Scotty up and kissed his cheek. "Buck is friends with them now?"

"Yes," Scotty said proudly, "but he's allowed in the kitchen. Them aren't. No way."

A warm fuzzy feeling came over her and she hated it. They were trying to break her. She'd smile for Scotty's sake, not because she wanted to. "Did they all come from the O'Neill's?"

"Yes, Mommy. They got *married* then they had Nino." Scotty put his face in front of hers. His eyes wide, he came closer and closer staring at her. He put his forehead against hers and just stared.

"I called Garrett. They'll be over later to lead them home," Stetson told her, plucking Scotty out of her arms. "Enough with the stares." He laughed.

"But Mommy needs to know that they are married."

"I think she knows, partner."

"Guess what, Mommy? Aunt Nellie wanted to know your favorite color and I told her you like orange best."

"Orange?"

"Yep. She has a surprise and she needed a color. I picked orange."

"I see." Looking at Stetson didn't give her any clues. "What's going on?"

"It's a surprise. Our son already told you, but don't worry, I knew that your favorite color is really yellow."

"You did?" she could feel her eyes filling. Stetson remembering touched her.

"I remember a lot about you." Stetson stepped close and wiped away a tear that had escaped. He grabbed her hand and while carrying Scotty, he led Storm inside. Buck took up the rear.

*****

Sneaky. That was the word of the day, sneaky. Storm wanted to hit someone. Everyone gave her little smiles, secret smiles. It was hard not to smile back at Scotty and Nellie, but Stetson and Joe got a scowl. They should know better.

She wasn't stupid; it had something to do with the supposed marriage proposal. Was there actually a proposal? Thinking back, she didn't think so. No flowers, no candy, no 'I can't live without you'. Nope. Nada.

Nothing. Yet she was supposed to be excited about them whispering.

Someone had to pay. They could not treat her this way. The problem was it was supposed to be all for her. Yeah right, it was for Stetson. He always had to get his way. Maybe she was being a bit uncharitable, but hell she wanted to scream.

"Storm?"

Storm stood at the corral watching the horses. She pretended she didn't hear Stetson's voice. She was half-afraid she'd turn around and sock him one.

"Storm?"

Storm turned and stared him down. "What? What do you need? What?"

"It's time for dinner." Stetson's eyes contained too much merriment.

"Go to hell."

"So, you're not hungry?" He had the nerve to smile at her.

"Listen, cowboy, if you smile at me one more time--"

Stetson put his arms around her and pulled her close. He ducked his head and took her lips. It was a long kiss, a deep kiss, a mind-blowing kiss.

"Stop it." Storm pushed him away, feeling a bit light headed. "You are such a brute."

Stetson smiled. "Oh really? You didn't seem to think so a few minutes ago."

"A simple lapse in judgment. It happens every five years or so."

"I love it when you're like this."

Storm gasped, narrowing her eyes. "Like what?"

"All feisty and sexy."

"I'm going to wipe that grin off your face, Stetson. Don't think I won't. For two days you've been smiling at me. Well a person can only take so much." Her heart beat faster and her breath became shorter.

"A smile. You get this worked up about a smile?"

Stetson's eyes widened in feigned surprise.

"You think you know it all. You can't waltz back into town, and expect it to be all right. I've changed. I'm not some little naive girl that believes everything you say." Storm turned away from him. She didn't want him to see her cry.

Stetson stepped behind her, and enclosed her in his arms. "I'm sorry, babe. Damn it, I did it all wrong again. I got caught up in all the fun, and I never asked you what you want. You're right. Go ahead and wipe the grin off my face. I deserve it."

Storm shook her head. "Stop trying to make me laugh."

"Why not? I love your laugh. I don't hear it very often."

"No, I don't suppose you do."

"Storm, will you--"

"No."

"I didn't even ask you yet. Will you go camping with me?"

She quickly turned in his arms and looked at his face to see if he was serious. "Camping?"

Stetson nodded. "The three of us. Let's see what it would be like to be a family. Please, Storm, give us a chance. That's all I'm asking for."

He smelled so good. He felt so good. Her heart pounded. She longed to be a family, but she was wary. Finally, she sighed and leaned her head on his chest. "Okay."

"Really?"

"Yes, really." She hoped that she wasn't making a mistake.

Stetson let go of her in a flash and ran toward the house calling Scotty's name.

It looked like she made two men very happy.

*****

Stetson wiped his brow and smiled when Scotty did the same. They had set up the tent, getting ready for the night to come. "Looks like the Scott men have made shelter for their woman." He winked at Storm and she rewarded him with stunned look and a shake of her head.

"Very macho, Stetson, but Scotty knows that woman can take care of themselves." She gave him a so there, smile.

"I like being a taco. Daddy and me, we are takin' care of you." Scotty plopped himself down in her lap and smiled at her.

Storm laughed and stroked Scotty's blond curls. "Yep, you two are tacos."

Stetson started to open his mouth to correct them, but there was no way he was going to dim Storm's smile. Heck, he was surprised she'd agreed to the camping trip. Hopefully it would lend itself to many opportunities to be close to her.

He smiled back. He had bigger tents, but he brought the two-man tent they had used on Sinner's Island. Closeness was the key. He'd break through her reserve somehow. "Who wants to go fishing?"

Storm gasped in pain as Scotty pushed off her lap and then jumped on it.

"I do. I do!" Scotty chanted.

Stetson grabbed him in mid jump and held him. "Careful of your mommy, cowboy."

"I forgot we are tacos with man strength."

"Man strength?" Storm rolled her eyes and got off the ground. "Well let's see who catches more fish, man strength or woman intelligence."

Stetson was thrilled to take on her challenge. She was beautiful with her blue eyes practically dancing. Her long blonde braid hung down her back. "Come on, let's get the gear."

"I'm going to be a fisherman when I grow up," Scotty

proclaimed.

"I thought you were going to be a cowboy?" Stetson led them to the placid lake.

"Oh this is a great spot." Storm scanned the lake.

"You used to come here."

Storm's eyes shadowed when she looked at Stetson. "Seems like another lifetime ago."

Grabbing her hand, Stetson pulled her toward him. He kissed her cheek and grabbed her rear, making her jump. She was smiling again, a good sign. "Come on, Scotty, we have to use our man strength, and show Mommy how macho we are."

"We're not tacos?"

Storm laughed loudly. "I need a little less talking. I don't want the fish to be scared away." She grabbed her pole and sat about ten feet from them. Gracefully she cast her line into the lake, leaned back against a tree, and sighed contently.

Storm appeared pleased and that could only be good news for him. He set Scotty up and helped him cast, receiving a grateful smile from her. Genius, that's what his camping idea was, pure genius. Smiles all around, what could be better?

After a few hours of fishing, Stetson and Scotty cleaned the fish she'd caught.

"Mommy is a good fisher."

"Well, Scotty, there is such a thing called beginner's luck."

Storm laughed. "Say what you will, I caught the most fish." Getting up, she started unpacking the pan and utensils they would need.

Dinner had been great with much laughter. Stetson hoped it made a difference to Storm.

It was a moonless night and the sky was dark. Cloud cover prevented the stars from shining through. Watching Scotty and Storm, Stetson could read the contentment on their faces. He'd helped Storm at every opportunity until he was afraid she was going to run from him.

What he hadn't planned on was his reaction to her closeness. She was driving him wild. The slightest brush against her and his body became aroused. He'd given her the grin of the devil each time, but he tried to think of anything but her. Counting backwards didn't help. Knowing that Scotty was right there didn't seem to dampen his need.

It was a campaign that he needed to see through to the end. God help him. There wasn't a cold shower in sight. Trying to imagine his parents in bed together finally helped but only slightly.

"Do you think it's going to rain?" Storm looked at the sky.

"No."

"How do you know?" Storm asked.

"Yeah, Daddy, how do you know? Do you have special powers?"

"Well, see..." He got up and sat between Storm and Scotty, making sure that his leg was touching Storm's. He heard her quick intake of breath and it made his body hum. "Look at those clouds. See how white they are? Those aren't rain clouds. Sniff the air, do you smell rain?"

Scotty sniffed and sniffed. "Nope, no rain."

"You can't tell by smelling." Storm moved her leg away from Stetson's.

"Mommy, if Daddy say's it's true then it is." He nodded his head emphatically.

Storm glanced at Stetson. Her gaze was anything but encouraging. "Right, kiddo. How about jammie time?"

"Nope." Scotty went right back to looking at the clouds.

"What do you mean no?" Storm asked.

"I have no wheres to sleep. Daddy only broughted one bag."

Storm turned to stare at Stetson. "What is he talking about?" Her voice sounded wary.

"I brought two that I turned into one big one."

"Well unmake them. Scotty and I will share one."

"Nope." Stetson smiled at her.

"And why not?"

"I thought we'd all hunker down together. You know, real camping." He gave her an innocent look.

"Mommy, lets hunker," Scotty jumped up. "Jammie time," he yelled, running into the tent.

"You're playing dirty, Stetson."

"I don't know what you mean." He turned his hands palms up, trying to portray his innocence.

"Well--"

Stetson swooped down and caught her lips with his. They hadn't had any time for kissing on their trip. She shook her head once, and then opened her mouth, allowing his tongue in. She tasted like pure heaven, chocolate, marshmallow, and graham crackers.

Storm put her fingers through his hair, and then she touched his cheeks before she moaned into his mouth. She pulled back and leaned her forehead on his chest, breathing heavily. "Wow."

Stetson smiled, wow was a good word. He stroked her back and kissed her temple. "There is nothing better than having you in my arms."

She pulled back until she could see his eyes and she stared. Finally, she smiled and nodded.

"I have my jammies on," Scotty yelled, from the tent.

Stetson got to his feet and held his hand out to help Storm. He pulled her up and close. "Time for some good old hunkering."

Storm laughed. "Scotty will be sleeping in the middle."

"Of course. I wouldn't have it any other way."

*****

Feeling cocooned and snuggly, Storm started to wake up. Something wasn't right. Opening her eyes, she turned her head and was surprised to find Stetson lying right next to her, wearing a cocky grin on his face. "What?"

"Shh, darlin'. Don't wake up the little tyke."

Storm didn't move. She realized that Stetson had one arm around her and one around Scotty. His tanned muscular arm. If she moved an inch toward him, she'd be lying with her head on his shoulder. His beautiful, broad shoulder.

"How did you end up in the middle?" she whispered.

"Scotty had to talk to a man about a horse."

"You didn't teach him that saying did you? I don't want to have to hear it twenty times a day."

"Ummm." Stetson kissed her forehead. "Maybe you'll just hear it ten times a day."

Trying not to smile was impossible. He always made her laugh. Before she knew it, she had her hand on his washboard stomach. He quivered, causing her to shiver.

"Scotty wanted me in the middle, so I figured why not?" Stetson's eyes twinkled knowingly at her. He gave her his slow sexy grin making her sigh.

"Morning, Mommy. Morning, Daddy," Scotty said, excitedly. He propped his head up on Stetson's chest and smiled. "Just like real mommies and daddies that sleep together."

"You know, you're right."

Storm scrambled out of the sleeping bag before Stetson said anything else. They might have chemistry, but that didn't mean they were getting married.

She quickly got dressed. She didn't even care who was watching. Grabbing her boots, she stomped out of the tent. Just who did he think he was?

Sitting on a tree stump, her anger turned into

disappointment and hurt. This whole pretense of wanting to be together and go camping was just a set-up. Tears filled her eyes. Was every kiss, every touch as calculated? How could she have believed? Once a fool always a fool.

Shoving her boots on, she got up and quickly started toward the pond. Her need to be alone propelled her forward. Suddenly she felt herself falling into the sharp rocks on the side of the path. Stunned, she just lay there wondering what happened.

Hearing Stetson and Scotty running her way she yelled, "Stop! I tripped on some wire. Be careful!"

Stetson told Scotty to stay where he was and then cautiously walked toward Storm. "Are you hurt?"

"Not seriously. A few scrapes. The wire was strung across the path."

Stetson swore and shook his head. "I'll need gloves and wire cutters to free you. Good thing you had your boots on."

Nodding, she watched them walk toward the campsite. It was crazy. Who would put wire up like that? This was Scott land.

"Got 'em, Mommy," Scotty yelled from his position.

Stetson approached and squatted down. His anger emanated off him making Storm wary.

"I shouldn't have run out of the tent like that."

Stetson stopped untangling the wire and looked at her. The concern in his eyes filled her heart and she bit her lip to keep from falling under his spell.

"I'm going to pull your boots off."

"Good idea." She was glad to have something else to focus on beside Stetson's sexy beard.

"Are you cold? I could have Scotty grab your coat."

"No, it was a shiver or a chill. I'm fine." She scrambled to her feet. "How did this wire get here?"

"Damned if I know, but I intend to find out."

Storm looked at the damage the wire had done to her boots. "What if it had been Scotty on this path? He'd..." Storm choked up.

Stetson scooped her up and held her tight. "Let's talk about it later. I'm as alarmed as you are."

"Mommy, are you all right?" Scotty yelled, jumping up and down, waiting for them to get closer.

"I'm tough, kiddo." Storm smiled at him.

"And the bestest fisher in the whole world."

Stetson laughed and she could feel the rumble of it against her body. "Yep that's your mom. I think we should break camp and head out. Hard to camp without boots on."

"Yes, really, really hard," Scotty agreed, leading the way back to the campsite.

Stetson pulled the truck in front of the house.

Storm had a smile plastered on her face, for Scotty's sake

Getting out of the truck, he strode to the passenger side door. He opened it and took Storm's hand. She cried in pain. "What on earth?" He looked at her palms. "A few scrapes? You have gravel imbedded in your hands. Damn it, Storm, you're bleeding."

Storm tried to brush him aside and get out of the truck. Stetson scooped her up in his arms. "Scotty, I'm going to put Mommy on the porch and then I'll get you out of your car seat."

"Really, I'm fine."

Plopping her down on the porch swing, Stetson touched her knee. His eyes narrowed at her cry of distress. "Not hurt, huh?"

"Just go get Scotty. I didn't want to scare him. He used to have nightmares that something would happen to me and he'd be all alone."

Stetson went back and retrieved his son.

"Is Mommy bad hurt?" The quiver in his voice became an arrow in Storm's heart.

"Not bad. You can help me fix her up."

"You said a bad word, Daddy."

Stetson appeared puzzled.

"You said damn. Damn is what you said. Damn is bad. Mommy, isn't damn bad?"

Storm laughed. "Yes, so quit saying it."

Scotty gave Stetson an, *I told you so* look.

"Both of you."

Scotty's eyes grew wide. "See Daddy, you got us both in trouble with your bad word."

"Scotty, can you get the door?"

Stetson scooped Storm up and carried her inside. Gently, he put her down on a kitchen chair. "Hey, I wonder where Nellie and Joe are. Joe's truck is outside."

"So is Nellie's car," Storm commented, biting her lip.

"Do you think?"

Storm nodded her head.

"They can't wait a few weeks until they get married?"

"I found them," Scotty yelled, from the top of the stairs. "They are wrestling just like the guys we watched on TV."

Storm doubled over in laughter. Her shoulders shook and tears poured down her face.

"Scotty, I need you." Stetson shook his head. "He'll be scarred for life."

They heard his footsteps as he ran down the stairs. "I'm ready. Do we get to oper, opra? Can we be doctors?"

"You most certainly are not going to operate on me. I want you to help Daddy. I might sound like I'm in pain, but it'll be fine." Holding out her palm, she showed him the rocks imbedded in her hand. "Daddy has to get these out. I'll try to be brave, but I'll probably need your help."

Scotty looked at Stetson. "Let's just knock her

out. I bet you can do it in one punch."

Stetson laughed and shook his head. "You know, that's a great idea, but my punches are so strong, I might hurt her."

"Oh. Mommy, you'll have to be brave."

Later that day, Storm looked around the dinner table, feeling blessed. Stetson and Joe cooked roast chicken and mashed potatoes. They also cooked some peas, but they didn't quite make it to the table. Smiling, she remembered the look of surprise on Stetson's face when Scotty dropped the bowl of peas on the kitchen floor.

Thank goodness, it had been a wooden bowl. She had gotten up to help clean the mess, but was ordered to relax. Scotty smiled; peas were not his favorite.

It felt so unnatural to be taken care of. Her emotions were on a seesaw. One minute she was angry and determined, and then the next she was all warm and fuzzy. There was something to say about warm and fuzzy. It felt damn good.

"Mommy, do you need me to feed you?"

Storm smiled. "I was wool gathering. I can eat, but thanks."

"Daddy, can Buck and me see the lamb?"

Stetson looked at each adult then at Scotty, clearly puzzled. "What lamb?"

Storm shook her head. "Scotty, wool gathering means thinking."

Scotty's shoulders slumped. "Oh." He ate a forkful of potatoes and turned toward Stetson. "Can we get a lamb?" His eyes were so big and hopeful.

Storm had been on the other end of that look often. Hiding her smile behind her napkin, she peered at Stetson.

A flash of confusion showed in his expression followed by awareness. Then there was the frown of no, and finally the look of 'what do I say to Scotty'. "I'll have to talk it over with your mom."

"Oh no. You are not putting this on me, cowboy. It's your ranch. You had no problem bringing home a puppy."

"Please?" Scotty's eyes got even bigger.

"Tell you what, Stamos has a few foals we can go visit."

"Fools are lambs?" Scotty eyes narrowed unconvinced.

"Foals are baby horses." Stetson looked defeated.

Storm expected him to cave at any moment. However, she was surprised when he held strong. It was hard with that cute little look of Scotty's. If truth were told, he never asked for much. There had never been anything to give, except love.

Joe brought out homemade brownies and both women were impressed.

"Got yourself a keeper," Storm commented.

Nellie nodded and smiled. "I think Stetson can make cookies." Her eyes twinkled.

"Well before anyone asks for any, I'm taking my son upstairs for a bath." Stetson smiled.

Joe stood up. "I'll do the dishes."

Storm and Nellie looked at each other in surprise. Nellie shrugged her shoulder. "Come on Storm, let's be women of leisure in the other room."

Storm followed Nellie into the big family room. She waited for Nellie to sit on the couch and then she joined her. "Wrestling?"

Nellie face turned bright red. "That was Joe. I was speechless. I do apologize."

"Oh no, don't apologize. Scotty shouldn't have gone looking for you in the bedrooms."

"He's always been invited to do so before. Next time we'll lock the door."

Storm laughed. "Good idea."

"I did hear a bit of gossip while you were away.

Your father's foreman, Smitty, left."

"Smitty's been Dad's right hand man since before I was born."

Nellie touched her arm gently. "Maybe left isn't the right word. No one seems to know where he went. Rumor has it he went for a ride and never came back."

Storm's heart dropped into her stomach. "I need to find out. Smitty taught me how to ride a horse. Where did you hear this?"

"Miss Harriett told me."

"Damn. Then it's probably true. She always has been sweet on him." Storm jumped up and grabbed her purse. "Can I borrow your car?"

"Where are you going?" Storm spun around toward Stetson.

"I, well, I guess I'm going into town to find Smitty. He's missing."

"Let me make a few calls first. I bet either Stamos or Garrett know what's going on." He walked right up to her and touched her cheek. "Trust me."

Storm wanted to shake her head no, but his beseeching eyes asked for so much. She saw love, concern, doubt, and hope. A lump formed in her throat. Perhaps it was time to trust Stetson. She nodded, staring deeply into his blue eyes.

Stetson leaned down and kissed her. It was the most tender kiss she had ever received. It touched her soul and left her speechless. He pulled away and she touched her lips, staring in awe.

Giving her one of his slow sexy grins, he turned and walked into the office.

Kathleen Ball

CHAPTER ELEVEN

Brushing down Bandit, Stetson was still mulling over what Stamos had told him last night. Smitty had been missing for at least a week, and no one reported it. McCrory supposedly searched for days before his men finally found Smitty's roan.

Sam Evers was the new foreman. Stetson never liked the guy. He was supposedly one of the men who claimed that Scotty could be his. Now McCrory wasn't allowing anyone but law enforcement on his property. It just didn't sit right.

Storm had been near hysterical last night. At least she accepted his comfort for a small while. The feel of her shapely body in his arms was something he wanted again and again.

"What do you think?" he asked the horse. "Yeah, I don't know what to think either. I guess I'll have to give her some space then launch another attack. Thing is, I just don't know what to do to make her trust me."

Bandit just gave him a baleful look. Hearing someone enter the barn, Stetson looked up. "Hey, Joe."

"Nellie wants your help in the kitchen."

"I was just about to take Rosie out to check the

west end of the ranch."

Joe shrugged his shoulders. "You know how Nellie gets."

Sighing, Stetson nodded. "I'd best get in there." He walked over and patted Rosie. "I'll take you out in a bit."

"Do you want me to ride out and check?"

Stetson shook his head. "No, I need you out with the other men, checking the cattle. I'll just be a second I'm sure." Stetson walked to the door and turned. "Joe, be careful out there. I don't like what's going on."

"Me neither, Boss."

Stetson walked toward the house. What could Nellie need him to do that she couldn't have asked Joe to do? He'd never understand women.

Nellie looked up from the bowl she was busy stirring. "Oh good, you're here."

Stetson nodded. Nellie had that pregnant glow about her and he had never seen her so happy. "What can I do for you?"

"I need the cradle brought down front the attic. I, well, you know what it looks like and I thought you could find it faster than me and..."

"I'll get it. I don't want you hurting yourself."

Nellie gave him a grateful smile.

"Be back in a second."

Standing on the landing leading to the attic, he noticed that the light was on. Nellie must have already searched. He'd have to tell her to stay out of the attic. She could easily trip and fall.

He opened the door and walked in. The delectable sight of Storm bending over greeted him. "I didn't know you were up here."

"Just looking for the cradle," she said, not even straightening up.

The sound of the door closing alerted them both. Walking to it, he tried to open it. It was locked. He shot Storm a puzzled look. "How'd it get locked?"

Storm brushed past him. "Let me try." Storm pulled at door handle to no avail. She banged her fist against the door and then listened to see if anyone heard her.

"I'll be back later. You two work out your differences or you'll stay in there indefinitely," Nellie told them, her voice betraying her happiness at her little plan.

"Nellie, you open the door right now!" Stetson roared.

All they heard were whispers, and the sound of her walking away.

"Is this really happening?" Storm stared at him.

"We might as well look for the cradle. Sounds like we'll be here for a while."

"Why? Because I don't want to marry you?"

Stetson ignored her and continued to look for the cradle.

"You do think it's my fault."

"Look, Storm, let's just find the cradle and wait for a bit. Someone will let us out."

Storm didn't look so sure. She walked to the window and laughed. Picking up a picnic basket full of food, she turned toward Stetson. "Looks like we'll be here much longer than you thought."

*****

The sight of Stetson's jaw drop made her happy. For once, he wasn't in control and obviously, he didn't appreciate it.

Stetson closed his mouth and scowled. "Anything good in that basket?"

Storm set it down on a sheet-covered table. "Water, beef jerky, and protein bars. Really, they shouldn't have been so generous. Why bother? Oh look, there's candles and a note."

Stetson stood beside her trying to read the note. "Well?"

She didn't know whether she should laugh or be mad. "It's a petition."

"What the hell?" Stetson took the paper out of her hand. "Even Buck signed this?" Stetson went to the door and banged loudly. "I have work to do, damn it."

"Pst. Damn is a bad word." A voice came from under the door.

Stetson was instantly on his stomach looking under the door. "Scotty, open the door, please."

Storm flew over and lay next to him. Scotty's eyes were wide and Buck was putting his black paw under the door. "Scotty can you reach the door handle?"

"Daddy said damn again."

"I know and he'll stand in the corner as soon as you open the door." Buck had rolled onto his back and was looking at them upside down. "Open the door, kiddo."

At the sound of approaching footsteps, Scotty and Buck scrambled away from the door.

"Damn, that sounds like Joe out there," Stetson roared.

"Daddy said damn."

Storm couldn't make out what they were saying, but the sound of footsteps walking away rang loud and clear. "Damn!"

Stetson rolled on his back, his arm over his eyes. "Don't say damn."

Sitting up Storm grabbed the note back. "So, looks like we have to announce our engagement to get out of here. That's simply not possible. I suggest we wait them out."

Stetson lifted his arm and looked at her. "For how long?"

"For as long as it takes."

Stetson sat up and leaned against the door. "I

suggest we just name the date and walk out of here."

"Oh you do? I don't agree, you unromantic oaf."

Running his hand through his blond curls, he gave her a long glance. "Let's get out the water, the jerky, and the candle. Would that be more to your liking?"

Standing up, she walked to the other end of the attic. Sunlight shone through the window displaying all the dust in the air. They'd be better off if they just stayed silent. He was in a mood and so was she.

Stetson stood but stayed by the door. "What? Not to your liking?"

Ignoring him, Storm looked for the cradle. There were several old trunks, boxes, and pieces of furniture. Most of the furniture was draped in sheets. In the corner, she found an old spinning wheel. "Oh look at this."

Stetson glanced at her and smiled. "That was great grand granny Betty's. I haven't been up here in years."

Storm smiled back until she realized she was smiling and turned away. She was here to find the cradle and nothing else. Scotty would want her soon and Nellie would have to open the door.

"It's hot in here."

Stetson nodded and walked toward the window. "Doesn't open."

"I noticed."

"Storm, this was not my idea so stop the sarcasm."

She felt a nagging of guilt. Maybe she was being a bit bratty. "Well I don't see the cradle. We might as well sit and relax. You can tell me about your rodeo days."

Stetson grabbed two bottles of water and handed her one. He uncovered a couple wooden chairs and offered her one. "Might as well be comfy."

Storm sat trying not to look at him. He was grinning again and for some reason it was her weakness.

She could feel his eyes on her and her body began to ignite.

"Not much to tell. I followed the circuit and made some money."

"Must have been more than that to keep you away for so long."

Stetson hesitated. "I didn't come back for two reasons. One was my father. The other was you."

"I'm not buying it so stop selling it." Storm took a bite of jerky.

"You think I'm lying?"

"Yes. I believe the part about your father, but don't put me down as a reason you stayed away."

Stetson stood up and walked toward her, making her scurry to the farthest wall away from him.

"Don't touch me, and while I'm at it, I'm sick of those sexy grins you keep giving me."

Stetson laughed. "My grins are sexy?"

"Stop where you are. You could have picked up the phone at any time. When you left, I was devastated. When you never called it near killed me. I was so stupid, I thought you loved me. I kept telling myself that you'd come back. I was such a fool."

Stetson took another step toward her and she felt cornered. Blindly striking out, she hit Stetson with her fist. His yelp of pain scared her.

He gave her an incredulous look and covered his eye. "You walloped me."

"I didn't mean it."

Stetson picked her up and put her over his shoulder. Her fists pounded on his back and he let her slide to the floor. He grabbed her and straddled her. "It hurts like hell."

"Aunt Nellie, come quick. They are wrestling and Daddy said hell," Scotty called from the other side of the door.

They both looked in the direction of the door and

saw a shadow. They stilled for a moment, and then Stetson pulled away from Storm.

"Scotty, I told you not to spy," Nellie said.

"Nellie, let us out of here right now," Stetson yelled.

"Daddy is mad."

"He might be a bit mad now, but he'll thank us later," they heard Nellie tell Scotty.

"She pun--"

Storm put her hand over his mouth. "Shh, don't let Scotty know I hit you."

"He already thinks we are wrestling," Stetson said, his eyes glittering.

"Now I already apologized for that little mishap. He saw us rolling on the floor and assumed we were wrestling."

"Yeah, but regular wrestling or Nellie and Joe kind of wrestling?"

Storm started to laugh, but when she looked closely at his eyes, she could see one start to color and swell. "Wow, I didn't know I could hit so hard."

"You sound impressed." Stetson touched his eye and winced.

Storm went and got one of the water bottles. "Here put this against it, maybe it'll help."

"Ouch, woman, that hurts." Stetson grabbed the bottle from her.

"I was just trying to help." Storm felt defensive; she couldn't do anything right.

They heard Buck scratching at the door. Then a piece of paper sailed through. Storm got up and looked at the paper. Tears filled her eyes.

"What is it?"

"Scotty drew us a picture."

Storm handed it to Stetson who smiled. It was a picture of a mommy, a boy, a daddy, and a dog, all in front of a house holding hands. "He has a point you know, Storm."

"I don't know what's what anymore," she confessed. Stetson reached out and pulled her onto his lap.

*****

Breathing in her scent, Stetson hugged her to him. Surprisingly, she leaned back against him and relaxed. It always seemed so right to have Storm in his arms. He kissed her neck and felt her shiver.

"What are we going to do?" Storm's eyes filled with doubt.

"I've tried every way I know how to make you trust me, Storm. I'm plumb out of ideas. I wish-- Never mind."

"No, tell me what do you wish?"

Her expression was so filled with hope. He prayed he had the words to tell her. Tucking her head under his chin, Stetson took a deep breath. He didn't want her observing him, viewing his heart and soul.

"I wish for you to be happy, and taken care of." He felt her try to look at him. "I know you can take care of yourself." She relaxed in his arms. "I just want to be there for you. I want to help you raise our son. I want you to look at me the way you used to. I want you to trust me. Most of all, I want you to love me as much as I love you."

Fear filled him as he waited for a response. The silence stretched out and his heart dropped. "I'd be so proud to have you as my wife. I understand, Storm. You don't have to say anything."

"I'm sorry, Stetson."

He kissed the top of her head and let her go. "I understand. The whole time I was gone I knew something was missing. I knew it was you. My damn pride got in the way. I foolishly went on with my life and pushed you and this place into the back of my mind. It's all my fault and I truly understand."

Storm stayed on his lap. Her eyes were luminous

when she finally gazed at him. "You're breaking my heart. I do want to marry you. I'm just hurt and afraid." Tears poured down her face.

"I want to make love with you. I want to show you that you don't need to fear me."

Reaching up, she stroked his beard. "I'm not afraid of you that way. I'm afraid you'll walk away again. I can't help it. It's always in the back of my mind."

Stetson wrapped his arms around her and rocked her back and forth. "It's down to trust. Tell me, what I can do?"

"Tell me that you love me again."

"Storm McCrory, I love you with all my heart. Please, marry me."

"All right."

"Aunt Nellie, it worked. Can I open the door?"

Kathleen Ball

CHAPTER TWELVE

Storm stared in the old Cheval floor mirror. It was a handsome mirror encased in cherry wood. It had been in the attic only yesterday and now it stood in her room. Her reflection astounded her. The wedding gown was beautiful. It was an A-line, short-sleeved confection with a square-cut neckline. The bottom layer was made of the softest satin she had ever felt with lace overlays. Nellie told her it was Venetian lace with hand-sewn seed pearls. The detailing on the bodice was exquisite.

Turning, she glanced over her shoulder. The fit was perfect. Nellie stood to one side wearing some flouncy yellow dress that if truth were told it made her look like big bird. Now she knew why her favorite color was of such interest.

"You are lovely, Storm," Nellie enthused.

Storm hoped her face projected happiness. She still felt a bit blindsided by the whole thing. If it had been anyone else but Nellie, she'd have put up a fuss. Getting married the day after accepting a proposal was not what she had in mind.

"Yellow looks nice on you, Nellie."

"Think so? I do love this dress. It's so sunny and

bright."

Storm watched as Nellie looked herself over in the mirror. Nellie actually liked the dress. Oh well, it was only for a few hours.

"I don't know why you went to all this trouble for a small wedding. It still is a small wedding, right?"

"Yes, it's small, and I went to the trouble because I love you."

Storm hugged her. "I love you too, Nellie."

A horn honked and Nellie smiled. "Come on, it's time."

Storm followed her down the old stairs her nerves getting the better of her. She longed to turn and run back to her room, but Scotty and Stetson were both waiting at the church for her, and she couldn't let Scotty down. Part of her wanted this marriage, but a bigger part thought it was a mistake.

Fear clutched at her heart and wouldn't let go. There was no doubt she loved that cowboy. She didn't doubt his love for her either. It should be so simple to go to the church, and walk down the aisle to the man she loved.

"Come on, Storm, our ride is waiting."

Storm hurried outside and stopped short. "What is going on?" She stared at the silver limousine parked in front of her.

Nellie smiled proudly. "It was my idea. We couldn't go in a truck."

"Of course not." Storm felt as though she was in some bizarre dream. She got in and settled her dress around her. "Thank you, Nellie, this is nice."

"Oh don't thank me, it was Stetson's idea."

"He decided yesterday and had it all arranged?"

"Not even Stetson could pull that off in such short notice."

"Nellie, how long has this all been planned?" Storm took a deep breath, trying to calm herself. It wouldn't be right to get Nellie upset.

Nellie's gaze flew to Storm's. She resembled a kid who was caught with her hand in the cookie jar. Her face was riddled with guilt.

Not wanting Nellie to turn any redder, Storm reached out and took Nellie's hand. "It's fine. Everything has been perfect, thank you." She concluded that she could torture Stetson tomorrow for his highhanded manipulations.

The limo stopped, and the driver helped Nellie and Storm out.

Callie came running down the steps with two bouquets of wild flowers in her hands. "Whew. Finally. Here you go." She handed them each their flowers. "I'm going in. You both look beautiful."

Joe came down the steps. His smile was only for Nellie. "They are waiting." He escorted both women up the steps and into the church.

Storm didn't even have a moment to think. The music started immediately. Joe and Nellie walked down the aisle. Now it was her turn. Looking at the end of the aisle, she saw Stetson and Scotty, both dressed in black tuxedos, standing, waiting for her.

Hearing the wedding march, Storm took a deep breath and started down the aisle. All doubts vanished when her eyes locked with Stetson's. She could feel his love in his look. Walking closer, she looked at Scotty, who was beaming. He waved to her. She winked back.

As she stood next to Stetson and Scotty, she knew all was right. The ceremony was a blur, but the kiss at the end was one she'd never forget. It was a kiss filled with love and promises.

Stetson lifted Scotty up so he could kiss her too. Storm thought her heart would burst. Her eyes filled with tears.

"I now pronounce you my Mommy and Daddy. My *married* Mommy and Daddy!"

Stetson laughed. He never looked more handsome. Reaching up, she stroked his bearded cheek.

"Too late to give the bride away, huh?"

Everyone turned and looked toward the church entry. Her father stood there looking beyond angry. Storm automatically took a step closer to Stetson.

"Please don't ruin this too," Storm said.

"Not me. The only one here to ruin you is that bum next to you. How do you get off to marry Storm when you have a woman with your child on the way sitting in my house?"

Stetson let go of Storm's hand, and handed Scotty off to Joe. He took a step forward, staring Patrick McCrory down. "I've already told you that I have never been with Chrissy in that way."

"She says you did."

"She's wrong. Now if you don't mind, I'm asking you to leave."

"Well whoever fathered Scotty fathered Chrissy's baby. We have the tests to prove it."

Storm's stomach began to roll. "What are you talking about?"

"I stole your son's hair brush. We went clear over to Fort Worth to get the hair and Chrissy tested. Sorry Storm, but once again this yahoo has made a fool out of you. He married you to get out of marrying Chrissy. It's not right."

Storm brought a shaking hand to her mouth in disbelief. "You're lying," she finally said.

"See for yourself." He flung a manila envelope across the floor. "I'll be waiting to hear from you, Stetson. Storm is already ruined. Chrissy's the one you should be concentrating on. Besides, when you go back to the rodeo, Chrissy will want to go with you. You won't be leaving your wife and child behind."

Storm gasped.

"He didn't tell you he was leaving? Here." He

threw a few flyers on the church floor. "This says it all." He turned on his heel and walked out.

Tears filled her eyes. She looked at Stetson, then Joe, and finally Nellie. No one reassured her it wasn't true. Lifting the hem of her dress, she ran out of the church. Her heart was in her throat as she jumped into the silver limo. The door opened and Nellie, Callie, and Joy all jumped in.

"Back to the ranch," Callie told the Limo driver as she took Storm's hand. "I'm so sorry, Storm."

"Well of course it's not true." Joy poured some whiskey into a crystal glass from the limo bar and handed it to Storm.

Nellie was awfully quiet. Storm felt bad. Who in their right mind wears a dress like that with bright yellow shoes unless she really wanted to please the bride? Her shoes -- there was one of the flyers stuck to the bottom. Storm grabbed it and smoothed it out.

She still had her doubts about Chrissy's claim, but she could no longer doubt Stetson planned to leave. The proof was right in front of her. Stetson's picture was even on the flyer for a rodeo in Wyoming. Her hands shook as she handed it to Nellie. "You knew."

Nellie nodded her head. "It was only going to be for the weekend and that was to be the end of his rodeo career."

She wished to God she could feel numb. The pain was excruciating, and she didn't know if she could bear it. It was just like before, only worse. He looked so handsome standing at the altar. Even his black eye looked good to her.

Never again. No man was worth it. "Do you think Joe could move into the house and I could move into his cabin?"

Nellie stared at her. "If that's what you want. But don't you want to talk to Stetson? I'm sure he can explain everything to you." Tears flowed down Nellie's face.

Callie reached over and gave Nellie a hug. "Don't cry. We need to support one another. Stetson might have valid reasons, but it's Storm's choice as to whether or not she's ready to hear them."

Joy smiled at Nellie. "I'd pour you a shot of whiskey too, but the baby."

Nellie gave them a half smile. "My brother is a knucklehead. Storm, I knew about the rodeo. That's why he wanted the wedding so soon. I thought he told you. I'm sorry."

"I feel like he's thrown our future away. I just don't know what to think anymore. I just know I'm a fool. I don't remember Scotty's brush being missing."

"It was, but then it showed up on the floor so I thought maybe Buck had taken it." Nellie bit her bottom lip as she looked at Storm.

"Today was supposed to be our new start. I'm right back where I was five years ago, broken hearted and ashamed. Thank you for riding home with me. I can't believe I left Scotty."

The limo stopped. "Stetson has Scotty, he'll be fine." Callie reassured her. "Let's get your things so you can stay at the cabin for a few days."

"I'd really just like to be alone for a bit. I'd appreciate it if you could stay with Nellie until Joe gets back." Storm climbed out of the limo. "I'm going to get changed, and then take Mitzi for a ride. Maybe I can clear my head. I just don't know."

"Go, don't worry, we'll keep Nellie company," Joy told her with a smile.

Storm nodded and raced into the house. The screen door echoed in the empty house. She ran along the wide planked wooden floor and up the stairs. Stopping in front of the full-length mirror, she admired her dress once more, and then quickly got out of it. She pulled on her riding clothes, and headed out.

*****

Stetson tore off his tuxedo jacket, threw it on the floor, and stomped on it. How did everything go so haywire? Storm's father needed a serious pounding.

The sight of her running away ripped his heart in two. He was so close to having it all. Storm and Scotty were all he wanted. Scotty had been inconsolable after Storm high tailed it out of the church.

Damn! Damn! Damn! He stomped the jacket again. McCrory had painted him a liar and a cheat. How was he going to get Storm to believe him? To trust him?

"Done?" Stamos stood at Stetson's bedroom door, the manila envelope in his hand.

"Not nearly."

"I've looked these results over and something isn't right. I'll have to make a few calls, and find out if I'm on to something." Stamos gave him a sympathetic look.

"I didn't even look at them. There is no possible way that I'm the father of Chrissy's baby." He leaned down and grabbed his jacket. "I always thought of her as a sister. Anything you can do to disprove her claim..."

Garrett ambled into Stetson's bedroom. "These flyers look pretty damning. You should have told her, buddy."

"Those flyers aren't legit. I'm receiving an award from the Rodeo Association and I'm guest hosting. The only thing right about those flyers is the date and place."

Nellie elbowed her way in. She looked around the room filled with vases of yellow roses. A wedding ring quilt adorned the big bed. "I thought Storm knew about Wyoming?"

"It was going to be a surprise. You already offered to take care of Scotty for the weekend and I thought it would be a mini honeymoon."

"Uh oh, big brother, you have some explaining to do to your bride."

Stetson grabbed her hand and sat her on the bed. "Aren't you going to ask about the paternity test?

Nellie shook her head. "I already know you are not the father. You said you weren't, and I believe you."

Stetson leaned over and kissed her cheek. "Thank you for that."

Nellie looked at Stamos and Garrett. "Your wives are waiting in the kitchen."

"Don't worry, well get to the bottom of this." Stamos shook Stetson's hand.

"You'll be honeymooning in no time," Garrett added.

Stetson gave them a quick nod and watched them leave his room. He turned to Nellie and took her hand. "Thanks for today. You made the wedding beautiful. Your dress is, um-- Storm loves yellow. I appreciate the roses and Grandma's wedding quilt."

"You know I love you and Storm. Everything will work out."

Joe knocked on the door. "Scotty is still sleeping with Buck by his side. I went to my place, but it's occupied."

Stetson's heart dropped. "Occupied?"

Nellie squeezed Stetson's hand. "Storm will be staying there for a while."

His stomach rolled. "What about Scotty?"

"I think it's probably best to have him over there with Storm." Nellie's eyes began to tear. "I know you'll get it all worked out." Standing up, she took Joe's hand, leading him out of Stetson's room.

His dreams shattered as he looked at all the yellow roses. Getting off the bed, he carefully folded up the quilt. He wouldn't need it for a while.

*****

"But why?" Scotty asked Storm for the hundredth

time. The distress on his little face wrenched her heart. Buck whined too. It was more than she could handle.

Joe had brought their belongings over last night, and he grabbed some of his to take to the main house. He hadn't said much, but the pity in his eyes caused a lump to form in her throat. It was still there.

"Is Daddy still my daddy? Do I have to give Buck back?" Tears poured down his little face.

Storm picked him up and sat him on her lap. "It's going to be all right, kiddo." Rocking him back and forth, Storm knew she was telling him a lie.

A knock at the door, had Scotty ejecting himself from her and hurling himself to grab the doorknob. "Daddy!"

Somehow, she wasn't surprised. Her coping skills had taken flight, and she wasn't ready to see him.

Storm gave him a brief glance as he walked into the kitchen with Scotty in his arms and Buck at his feet. "I'm taking Scotty for the day. Nellie is upset and it's not good for her. Do you think that you could spend the day with her?"

The pain in her heart was almost too much to bear. Storm simply nodded. She still couldn't look at him. The fear of becoming hysterical kept her silent.

"Run and get you boots, hat, and a jacket," Stetson told his son.

"Storm, I know we need to talk, but I don't think you'd listen to anything I had to say. I'm asking that you allow me to spend time with Scotty and I'm hoping you are willing to help at the house. Nellie really doesn't look good."

The regret in his voice washed over her. The lump in her throat felt even bigger. Nodding, she still refused to glance at him. For her own sanity, she couldn't. All she wanted was to rail and scream at him. Another black eye wasn't out of the question, but she couldn't with Scotty in the house.

"I'm ready, Daddy." Scotty raced over and gave her a big hug and kiss. "See ya later."

"Have fun." Trying to sound cheerful was difficult.

The door closed and Storm was alone. Logically, she knew Chrissy's baby was not Stetson's. Her heart knew it was a lie. The Wyoming rodeo hurt her beyond measure. He had planned to leave and that she couldn't forgive.

Taking a shower made her feel a bit better. She got dressed and tried to pull herself together. Being the cause of Nellie's distress weighed heavily on her. She'd spend her days at the house with Nellie and her nights at the cabin.

Storm didn't have to look far for Nellie. She sat on the front porch looking like she'd lost her best friend. Her eyes were red and her face was puffy. Her misery appeared soul deep.

"Oh, Nellie, you look like I feel."

Nellie gave her a ghost of a smile. "Have you looked in the mirror lately?" Her smile vanished. "I made a mess of everything."

"Come on inside." Storm helped her up from the chair. "We'll have a cup of tea. That always makes us feel better."

Nellie followed. "I think whiskey would work better."

Storm led her to a kitchen chair, and had her sit. "I don't think whiskey is the key. And before you say anything, I want you to know that I cannot, I will not talk about Stetson. Your friendship means too much to me."

"We're sisters now." Nellie's eyes watered.

Grabbing a tissue, Storm handed it to Nellie. "Yes, we are. I think I'll have some type of breakdown if we discuss yesterday. I do want to thank you for all that you did. The limo, my beautiful dress, wearing my favorite color."

Nellie blew her nose. "I'm thankful orange

wasn't really your favorite color."

Storm filled the kettle at the deep sink. "I just need some time to sort everything out and I want to keep it between me and your brother."

"No whiskey?"

Storm smiled. "No whiskey and no caffeine. I'm going to make sure your baby is healthy."

Nellie nodded. "You're not going to leave, are you?"

Storm didn't have the heart to mention she had nowhere else to go. "I'm going to help you during the day and sleep at the cabin at night. By the way, how did Joe take being moved out of his place?"

Nellie blushed. "It's easier to sneak around at night, and we don't have to pretend we're wrestling."

Joe walked in and grabbed a mug. He poured himself a cup of coffee. "Nothing wrong with a little wrestling," he said, winking at Storm.

"Why aren't you out working?" Nellie asked.

Joe bent down and kissed Nellie's lips. "Just wanted to make sure my best girl was feeling all right."

Storm envied the sheer joy on Nellie's face. Her stomach clenched. That should have been her and Stetson. Turning away, she grabbed the scarred wooden counter for support. No one said life was easy, but no one said it'd be so darn hard.

The whistling of the teakettle got her attention, and she busied herself making tea. She walked toward the table and put two teacups on it. Joe was giving Nellie another kiss and her heart twisted.

"You two gals have a good day." Joe went out the front door humming to himself.

Storm spent the whole day looking over her shoulder. Scotty and Stetson could come back at anytime, and she needed to brace herself. Her nerves were pulled taunt, and she felt as though she'd break.

With Nellie's help, she'd been able to keep

occupied. It didn't stop her thoughts though. Part of her was angry and a part of her felt worthless. Hard as she tried to hold on to the anger, doubts about herself kept creeping into her thoughts. Maybe Stetson just married her for Scotty's sake. He planned to leave the very next weekend. She didn't give too much credence to Chrissy's claim. Hopefully Stamos was looking into it.

"You know staring out the window isn't going to make them get here any faster."

Storm smiled at Nellie. She looked much better, and they'd had an almost nice day of avoiding the topic of Stetson. There had been plenty of times Nellie would just stare at her, wanting to say something. Thankfully she didn't.

She heard the horses before they came into view. Scotty looked radiant. Whatever it took, for Scotty's sake, she reminded herself.

"Mommy! We chas-ed little cows. They are called halfs. They are half a cow."

Storm lifted him into her arms and gave him a big hug. "I'm glad you had a good day."

"It was the best ever. Right, Daddy?"

Stetson laughed. "Calf, not half. We sure did have a good time."

He looked at Storm and held her gaze. She could see he was hurting too. Giving him a weak smile, she set Scotty down and told him to get washed up for dinner.

"Storm--"

"Not now. Not with our son around."

"I never slept with Chrissy."

"Stetson, I know that. I can't talk about it now. I feel raw inside and I don't want to say something I'll regret, for Scotty's sake. Let it be, please?"

Stetson's love filled his eyes, and she couldn't take it. Turning away, she walked into the kitchen to check on dinner. Her hands shook and her heart felt as though it had been ripped out and stomped on. Taking slow, deep breaths, she was able to get dinner on the table.

Kathleen Ball

CHAPTER THIRTEEN

Cattle were missing. Not a great number, but enough for Stetson to become suspicious. His neck felt stiff, and his shoulders felt as though he carried the weight of the world on them. He turned Bandit toward the canyon at the edge of his property.

Joe checked yesterday, but it wouldn't hurt to look again. It was strange how one day he could feel so happy and the next his happiness was ground to dust. At least he still had Scotty. There was an empty space in his life. The very space that Storm belonged.

She had quickly returned to the cabin last night after dinner, allowing Scotty to stay for another hour. Stetson walked Scotty to the cabin door, his heart pounding. He hoped for the slightest bit of encouragement, but his hopes were dashed.

Storm stood behind the door and closed it in his face. Rejection hurt. How the hell had everything gone so wrong? Storm even admitted that she didn't believe that he had slept with Chrissy. He had allowed her belief to give him optimism for forgiveness and understanding.

He still planned to go to Wyoming. He just had

to find a way to convince Storm to come too. Both she and Scotty. He shook his head realizing he hadn't a clue how to achieve it.

She wasn't the only one hurting. Her mistrust tore a piece of his heart out. He'd thought having her at the house would be a good thing, but it devastated him every time she avoided his gaze.

"Come on Bandit, we have cattle to find."

He rode into the canyon and found hoof prints but no cattle. Sighing, he realized he had a big problem. Getting out his phone, he called Joe.

"Better have some of the men fence this canyon off. I don't know if they are being held here then driven off, or if there isn't a back way through this canyon."

"Sure, Boss. I might have heard about old trails in that canyon, but I never saw any," Joe told him.

"I'm heading in. I want to teach Scotty more about horses."

"Okay, talk to you later."

Stetson put his phone in his jeans pocket. His whole chest felt heavy. Nothing was going right. Should he give Storm space? Should he be in her presence as much as possible? For once, he was at a complete loss as to how to get her back. This whole thing had been wrong from the beginning. He shouldn't have tried to make her mind up for her. She was more than capable to run her own life.

Stetson felt weary, older than his years. What he wouldn't give to have the right to kiss and hug his wife. Talk about a letdown. He'd been dreaming of their wedding night. His head hurt with all of his thoughts swirling continuously in his head.

"Bandit, let's head home, boy."

*****

"Come on, Scotty." Storm tried to keep them moving toward the house despite Buck's tendency to investigate everything in his path, taking Scotty with him.

"Do you think I can go to work with Daddy again?"

"I have no idea, but you do know that you can't go with him every day."

Scotty nodded. "Me and Ph-uck will have to help you sometimes. Daddy said so."

Her heart squeezed painfully, and she tried to smile at Scotty. Thankfully, Nellie had the door open and Scotty went racing toward her with Buck right behind him. Taking a deep breath, Storm followed.

Nellie had a determined look about her. A look Storm knew she should dread. Finally, they were going to have the talk. Storm wondered how to head her off. It was all too much. Her heart ached constantly and her mind wouldn't give her peace.

"Where's Daddy?"

"He had to leave early. You know what it's like being a cowboy." Nellie touched the brim of Scotty's hat.

He puffed up with pride. "Yes, cowboys have a rough life."

Storm smiled. "Let's get breakfast started."

"Everything is ready. Scotty eat up, Joe is taking you to town with him."

"Yes." Scotty ran for the kitchen.

"Before you object, we need to talk. I promise it will be a good talk." Nellie hugged her. "No arguing with the pregnant lady."

Storm nodded. She wanted to smile, but it just wasn't in her. Butterflies swarmed in her stomach, and her hands shook.

It was a challenge to get through breakfast. Storm didn't eat much. Scotty chattered as usual. Finally, he and Joe left. Storm wished she could go too.

"Let's go sit on the front porch." Nellie grabbed her teacup and started out the front.

Feeling as though she had no choice, Storm

followed. It was a glorious day, not too hot and not too cold. The sun had risen above the hills making the world seem to be a cheerful place. Too bad, she knew better.

"I'm not sure we should discuss this, Nellie. I don't want to be mad at you in any way."

"I have a feeling you will be thanking me. You'd know already if you and Stetson weren't so stubborn." She took a folder paper out of her pocket and handed it to Storm.

Storm's eyes grew wide as she looked at the flyer. "This isn't the one I saw before."

"I know. This is the real one."

Her eyes misted as she shook her head. "He wasn't leaving?"

"No."

Storm stood up and ran for the bathroom, where she promptly got sick. She splashed her face with water and looked in the mirror. All she saw was a fool. A weak, pathetic fool. How was she going to be able to face Stetson? She all but called him a liar.

She was instantly sick again until her stomach was empty. No wonder Stetson left early; he probably couldn't stand the sight of her. He must have felt sorry for her. He allowed her to stay on the ranch out of pity.

Why was life so hard? Is it only when a person is a child that they have happiness? She quickly dismissed that reasoning. Nellie and Joe were happy. Storm didn't know what to do.

Nellie knocked on the bathroom door. "Storm, are you all right?"

The concern in her voice was Storm's breaking point. Tears poured down her face. Grabbing a handful of tissues, she opened the door.

Nellie led her to the old leather couch and sat next to her, holding her as she sobbed.

*****

Wringing her hands, Storm paced inside the small cabin. It was an old, one-story structure with a big room for cooking and sitting, and two bedrooms in the back. Joe hadn't left his mark on it. There were no pictures or homey touches anywhere. It seemed so generic, but Storm was grateful for a roof over her head.

She wrapped her arms around her middle, trying to hold herself together. Her heart hadn't stopped palpitating since Nellie showed her the flyer. She knew that if not for Scotty, Stetson would have thrown her off the ranch. No one would blame him.

Her heart felt shredded. Why would her father go to such lengths? The little girl inside her, wanted to know what she had done. The woman she was now, wanted to know how anyone could be so hateful.

Stetson probably hated her. The first hint of trouble and she bailed on him. She felt washed in shame. What kind of wife leaves after the wedding and refuses to talk to her husband?

Nellie said she'd send him over as soon as he got back. She was keeping Scotty and Buck until Storm and Stetson talked.

What if Stetson didn't want to talk to her? She couldn't blame him. Oh God, he was walking toward the cabin. The urge to run and hide became overwhelming, but she couldn't do that to him.

Opening the door before he knocked, Storm drank in the sight of him. His golden blond hair appeared as though he'd been running his fingers through it. There were circles under his eyes, but it was his eyes that caused her sharp intake of breath. The pain she saw in them nearly killed her. It was her fault.

"Nellie said you wanted to talk to me?" His voice was gruff.

She reached out, took his big calloused hand, and pulled him into the cabin. It hurt to know she was the reason he looked like hell. "I feel as though I've lost my best friend," she whispered, not taking her eyes off his.

Stetson's Adam's apple moved up and down. He looked down at her hand, and then he met her gaze. "I know the feeling." He sounded so sad it hurt her heart.

"I know it's my fault, and I also know you probably can't forgive me. I never gave you a chance to explain. I never..."

Stetson's comforting arms went around her and pulled her close. Storm laid her cheek on his hard chest and closed her eyes, relishing the feel of him. This might be the last time he held her like this and the thought caused her to make a noise of distress.

Stetson pulled away and gazed at her. "We need to talk."

She followed him to the threadbare green couch. Sitting, she felt as though she had been sent to the principal's office and was awaiting her fate. Her legs shook and she put her hands on her knees trying to still them.

"I'm so sorry, Stetson. I shouldn't have run out on you. I never seem to get anything right. My life has been one disaster after another."

"Don't take all the blame, Storm. Your father and Chrissy caused this. I wish I had told you about Wyoming. I wish you trusted me not to leave you."

The despair in his eyes was too much. She broke out sobbing. "I'm sorry."

Stetson drew her to him. "I'm the one who needs to apologize, not you. I'm the reason you don't trust me. That's all on me. I wanted to surprise you with a trip to Wyoming. Nellie had already volunteered to watch Scotty."

"I feel like such a fool. How could I have believed my father? How did he fake the DNA test?"

Stetson looked into her eyes. He seemed to be searching for something. "You believed me?"

"Of course I believed you. You're not that type

of man."

"But I'm the type that would leave you?"

"You're going to have to realize I'm scared to death that you'll leave me. I thought I had worked through it. I thought it was behind me, but it's not."

Stetson's expression softened. "I love you enough to overlook that little flaw."

Storm almost protested, but Stetson had his lips on hers. It felt like a healing of sorts. She knew it would take time, but she could feel the start. It was a sweet kiss, a tender kiss, filled with love.

"I love you too. I want us to be a family." Storm could hear the longing in her voice.

"We'll get through this. We'll just take it slow. How about taking a trip to Wyoming with me?" Stetson's eyes smiled at her.

"I'd be honored to accompany you."

CHAPTER FOURTEEN

It'd been a long three days since their talk. Storm decided that she'd move back into the house when they got back from Wyoming. Stetson wished it had been otherwise, but he let her have her way. No sense in getting her feathers all ruffled.

The drive seemed longer than usual. Probably because of the awkward silence. Every time he glanced over at Storm she smiled back, but she didn't make any conversation. He didn't know what to make of the whole thing.

Once in Wyoming, Stetson headed straight for the rodeo grounds and got Rosie and Bandit settled. He might not be riding in the rodeo, but he would be riding in the ceremonies and his horses deserved accolades too.

"You miss it." Storm stroked Bandits head.

"It was my life for about five years, but I have something better now."

Storm gave him a curious look. "What's better than the rodeo?"

Stetson wanted to stomp his feet. She still didn't understand. "You, Storm. You are better than the rodeo."

"Oh, you mean because of Scotty."

"Thick sculled comes to mind, but I don't think you'd like me calling you that." Stetson moved behind her, wrapping his arms around her waist. "You. I love you," he whispered into her ear, and then proceeded to kiss the side of her neck, causing her to shiver.

Storm was silent. He turned her in his arms so he could see her eyes. She still looked confused.

"The fact that I love my son is a given. Loving you is a choice. Well actually, it isn't a choice. My heart would break without you."

Finally, a look of dawning came over her and she blushed. "I'm sorry. I'm just an insecure ninny."

"No, you are my beautiful, loving wife." Stetson framed her face with his hands. He angled his head and slowly he took her lips. Her sigh of contentment filled his heart with joy. They'd be all right.

"Hey, bud!" Brian yelled from the other side of the stables. "I was told that you weren't coming."

Giving Storm's nose a quick kiss, he let her go. "Now who would spread a nasty rumor like that?" he joked.

Brian looked serious. "My sister."

"Oh." Stetson didn't know what to say. They'd been best friends for so long and he didn't want Chrissy to come between them.

"Miss McCrory," Brian greeted tipping his hat.

"It's Mrs. Scott now." Storm smiled at him.

Brian's eyes flew to Stetson's. "Now wait a minute. How can you be married and engaged to my sister?"

"I was never engaged to Chrissy. Where'd you hear that?"

"Somewhere between her getting pregnant and her showing me the paternity tests. You are a low down dirty--"

"It's not my baby."

Brian charged at him, sending Stetson flying into a stall door. Stetson pushed right back sending Brian a few feet away. Storm tried to get in between them and suddenly she was on the dirt floor under Brian.

Stetson reached down and pulled Brian off his wife. She looked stunned and in pain. He dropped to her side anxiously. "Where does it hurt?"

"I feel like I've been run over by a truck."

"I'm sorry," Brian said.

"Go find the Doc." Stetson didn't even wait for a reply. "It's going to be okay. Anything feel broken?"

"I don't know." Storm tried to sit up and immediately laid back. "My head, shoulder, and ribs seem a bit painful."

"Damn, this is all my fault."

Storm reached out and caressed his bearded cheek. "This is Chrissy's fault."

If he hadn't already loved her, he would have fallen in love with her all over again.

*****

It was a long wait. Storm felt safe with Stetson by her side. Her back and head were throbbing. She'd hit the dirt pretty hard. Darn, Brian was powerful. Why she thought she'd be able to get them to stop fighting was beyond her.

All the commotion had brought a big crowd. Out of the corner of her eye, she could have sworn she saw that witch, Chrissy. Why wouldn't she just slink away and leave Stetson alone? Didn't Chrissy have any pride?

"You're worried."

"Of course I am. Sure nothing's broken?"

Storm nodded. "My head hit the ground and the left side of my back, right under the shoulder blade, must have hit a rock or something. Hurts to move."

"That's why I'm here." An older cowboy with a black bag knelt beside her. "Never thought to have to patch up your wife," he said to Stetson. "I've sewn your husband back together a time or two."

"Storm, this is Bones."

Her eyes widened. She wanted to make some type of joke, but in Texas, you didn't kid a man about his name. "Nice to meet you. You do tiny, even, stitches. Stetson's lucky to have had you sew him up."

Bones blushed. "Now tell me where it hurts."

"My head and back." Storm went on to explain her pain. Once again, she saw Chrissy out of the corner of her eye, just standing on the fringe of the crowd.

"Carry her to the medical facility, and I'll check her out. I don't think it's anything serious," Bones instructed Stetson. He waited while Stetson scooped her up. "So you're to be honored tonight. Congrats."

Stetson looked too concerned to smile. Storm knew the second he spotted Chrissy. His eyes narrowed and his jaw clenched. "You all right? I'm not hurting you am I?"

"No, Stetson, you're a comfort to me."

Stetson followed Bones to the medical tent and placed her on an examining table. She cried out in pain. Her back felt as though sharp knives were going into it.

"Stetson, go catch a breath of fresh air. I'll come get you in a few."

Stetson looked at her. He leaned forward and kissed her lips. "I'll be right outside."

Storm watched him leave. She hoped that he wouldn't run into Chrissy right now. His temper was too hot.

*****

Staring off into the distance, Stetson took in the beauty of the Grand Tetons. The mountains were majestic and awe inspiring. He had hoped to enjoy these Wyoming delights with Storm.

The sights and sounds of the rodeo made him smile. He'd missed the atmosphere, but he'd found more with Storm. He only had to convince her of that. Despite their reconciliation, he knew she still harbored a few doubts. He wanted to be the one to chase those doubts from the depths of her eyes.

Brian rounded the corner and Stetson stiffened. "How's Storm? I never-- I'm more sorry than I can say."

Stetson nodded. He didn't blame Brian. He blamed Chrissy. "It's not my kid."

"I have a DNA test that says different."

"Did you look at it? I mean really look at it?"

Brian shook his head. "I read the results. That's all I needed to see."

Stetson sighed and reached into his back pocket, pulling out his copy of the test. "Look closely. The DNA from both samples is exactly the same."

"Sure, that proves that you and the baby are the same."

Stetson shook his head. "We'd have some of the same markers, but they couldn't be exactly the same. You have to account for two different mothers."

Brian's brows furrowed over his hazel eyes. "What does that mean?"

"Both samples are Scotty's. From what I've read, they won't take a sample from a pregnant woman until she's about fifteen weeks along."

Brian's eyes grew wide, his jaw dropped open, and his face turned red. "She lied? The whole thing has been a lie?"

"Looks that way. I know she's your sister, but something's not right with her. She's not the same little girl I left a couple months ago."

"I haven't seen her."

Stetson put his hand on Brian's shoulder. "She was at the stables during the fight. Storm and I both saw her."

"Oh hell. I'm so sorry, Stetson. You've been like a brother to me and I accused you of getting my sister pregnant. I don't know what to say."

"Don't beat yourself up about it. Go find her and talk to her. Oh and Brian, good luck in the rodeo tomorrow."

"I have a great chance since you won't be riding."

Stetson smiled. "Well, anything to help."

"Will you still be attending the 'we love Stetson to death' dinner tonight?

Stetson laughed. "I'm going to try."

*****

Storm watched all the activity around her in astonishment. Setting up for a rodeo looked like hard work. There were so many horses, about a dozen bulls, and hundreds of cowboys. Each seemed to be busy.

Storm had one of the best seats in the stands and she was even provided with a pillow to sit on. Still she was in pain. So far, it hadn't been the honeymoon she had hoped for. She'd been looking forward to their nights together. Her hurt back put an end to those thoughts.

She was depressed. She had missed the awards dinner last night. Stetson had wanted to stay with her but she insisted that he go. He deserved to go to a dinner held in his honor.

She'd taken a pain pill and was soon in a deep sleep. She hadn't even heard Stetson come in. She had to admit that it was nice to wake up next to him this morning. If it hadn't been for her back, she would have made up for lost time. Stetson looked so sexy sleeping.

He had to help her shower and dress and it had been sheer torture to look and not touch or be touched. Parts of her were still on fire.

She'd been looking forward to a behind the

scenes look of the rodeo. She planned to meet all his friends. Sighing, she realized she should be grateful she was able to be there at all.

The view of the Grand Tetons was something she'd never get tired of looking at. The leaves on the aspen trees were beginning to turn yellow. Wyoming was beautiful.

Looking across the arena, she spotted Stetson watching her. She smiled and waved and it warmed her heart to have him do the same.

The stands began to fill up and she felt beautiful as cowboy after cowboy tipped his hat to her and said howdy. It had been a long time since she was treated with such respect.

She'd been so busy taking it all in she didn't notice Chrissy sat next to her until she was painfully jostled. Storm was amazed at the gall of that woman.

Slowly she turned her neck to glare at her. "There are plenty of seats still open, take one of them."

Chrissy smirked at her. "Here is fine. It's where I want to be. I can't wait for Stetson to ride in the opening ceremonies. He'll be searching for me so he can tip his hat to his special gal."

"Good to know. I'll be waiting for him to tip his hat at me, his wife." She saw a flicker of hate in Chrissy's eyes.

"So you left the little bastard at home. Stetson probably didn't want to explain to his friends how you roped him into marrying you."

"Roped?" Storm put all her energy into staying calm. She knew she was being baited.

"Oh come on, Storm. Everyone knows that you tricked Stetson. Just because your bastard has blond hair doesn't mean he's Stetson's. Why, I know at least ten other men who claim the kid to be theirs."

Chrissy's voice traveled and soon everyone around them had stopped and stared. The looks were all filled with condemnation. They probably all knew Chrissy; she was one of them.

Storm stared straight ahead. She'd been in this situation before. She'd been stared at, and called a liar; it wasn't new to her. It hurt, but she couldn't let any weakness show. People could be vultures, and any show of weakness was riveting to them.

"I don't know what you did to steal my man. Stetson is the father of the baby I'm carrying. It's me he loves." Chrissy might as well have been using a megaphone. Everyone heard her now.

Storm decided to ignore her. She really had no other option at the moment. She could hardly move. There was no way she could defend herself in this crowd. She could endure it. She was strong, she hoped.

Finally, the people around them settled down. Occasionally she was on the receiving end of a nasty stare. Try as she might, she couldn't figure out why Chrissy was doing this. Why? What did she hope to gain? Maybe she just wanted Stetson.

Storm glanced at Chrissy. She looked too happy. She did look pretty. Her thick, brown hair was loose and wavy down her back. Her brown eyes sparkled. "So how's the morning sickness been?"

Chrissy turned and looked at her. The surprise mixed with a bit of confusion in her eyes gave her away. "Fine."

"I found that coffee first thing made it disappear," Storm lied.

Chrissy smiled. "Me too, keeps the morning sickness away. No one had to tell me, I just knew. I'm a natural mother."

"What time do you feel the worst?"

"Time?" Storm could practically see the wheels turning in Chrissy's head. "I'd have to say between five and six in the morning. Peter, your dad, brings me coffee. He makes great coffee."

Storm gave her a short nod and looked toward the arena. Chrissy wasn't pregnant. Her father never made coffee. He had Cookie, who did all the cooking for him and the men. Storm remembered when she first realized she was pregnant. The smell of coffee made her sick. Morning sickness wasn't always in the morning either. She'd had her suspicions, but now she felt confident Chrissy wasn't pregnant.

The opening ceremonies began. The National Anthem was played. Everyone stood but her. The pain in her back prevented her from standing. She received more nasty stares. These people didn't know her. Yet they felt they could judge her.

Finally, the spectators sat down and Stetson rode into the arena riding Rosie. He looked so damn good in his new jeans, black boots, blue shirt, and dove gray Stetson hat. Storm felt proud as he rode the perimeter of the arena waving. He stopped Rosie in front of the section she was sitting in and he smiled at her, tipping his hat.

Chrissy stood up and blew him a kiss. "I love you too, Stetson!"

The look of horror on Stetson's face almost made the last hour worth it.

Chrissy sat back down. "Look didn't you get a program?" She showed Storm the glossy covered program with Stetson's picture on it. "Got mine signed!"

Storm took a second look. It was signed *To: Chrissy. I love you -Stetson.* "Nice. I'll have to get one." The signature wasn't Stetson's. Storm grew anxious. Chrissy wasn't mean, she was really crazy. Crazy made her more dangerous.

Chrissy's eyes narrowed as she stared at Storm. "It doesn't bother you that Stetson writes me love letters?"

"That is not a letter. Stetson is his own man. He's free to be friends with you if he wants. I know he's thought of you as a little sister for all the time he was traveling the rodeo circuit."

Chrissy's laugh sounded as though she was on the verge of hysteria. "Little sister? Oh, Storm, don't delude yourself. Just remember I know all about daddy dearest. You don't want that to get out, do ya?"

Storm didn't get a chance to answer. She saw Stetson walking toward her. He was making his way up the steps to her. Chrissy jumped up, bumped Storm out of the way, and threw herself into Stetson's arms.

Storm would have laughed at Stetson's stunned expression, but Chrissy had knocked her so hard, her back felt on fire. The pain was so intense she was hard put to take a deep breath.

The crowd hooted and whistled as Chrissy crawled all over Stetson. Chrissy had thrown her arms around his neck and she had her legs wrapped around his waist. Stetson was busy moving his head back and forth, trying to elude her kisses.

Storm had expected to feel jealous, but she didn't. She knew in her heart that Stetson loved one woman, her. She was confident in his feelings for her. In fact, when he looked at her with his eyes bugging out, she laughed.

The laugh made her back hurt all the more but she couldn't stop. The harder Stetson tried to pry her arms from his neck the harder she held on. Chrissy had one heck of a hold on him. Finally, Stetson set her away from him.

He immediately he was at Storm's side. "I..."

Storm smiled up at him. "I know. Can you help me up? I want to kiss my handsome husband."

Stetson immediately scooped her up and planted a passionate kiss on her lips. Her lips still tingled when he pulled away. He gently put her back down on her seat and sat next to her.

"Has she been giving you a hard time?"

Storm winked at him. "Of course, but let's not allow her to ruin our day."

*****

Squirming this way and that, Storm seemed to be trying to find a comfortable position. The thin line her lips made was all Stetson needed to see.

"Put your arms around my neck."

"Why?" Storm asked.

"I'm taking you to the hotel." Stetson was relieved when she finally nodded and reached for him. The way she was biting her lip had him worried. She was going to make herself bleed.

He lifted her carefully, yet she cried out when he brought her body in close to his. "I'm sorry," he whispered as he kissed the top of her head.

"It's okay." The pain in her wobbly voice tore at him.

A few people gave them glares, but most called out congratulations to him. He felt sad for Storm. She didn't deserve to be glared at. He was going to have to talk to Brian and Chrissy together. The whole situation was absurd and it had to stop.

He carried her to his truck, and an older cowboy rushed to open the passenger side door for him. "Thanks, Bub. I'm going to miss you."

Moisture filled the man's eyes. He waited until Stetson had settled Storm into the truck. "Keep in touch, ya hear? It's been a wild ride."

Stetson took the man's hand and shook it. "You know where I'll be and my offer stands. I could use a seasoned cowboy on my ranch."

Bub grunted. "An old timer you mean."

"Doesn't matter. You've been like a father to me and I'd feel honored if you came down to Texas to live."

Bub smiled his weathered face showed a lifetime of wrinkles. "I'll be down by and by. Maybe sooner than later."

"Take care, Bub."

"You too, partner. You take care of your little filly

there. I take it she's the one you've been pining for all this time?"

Stetson smiled, and nodded his head. "How you know so much is beyond me. Yes, she's the only one for me."

"Well don't keep her waiting."

Stetson watched Bub walk away. His limp was more pronounced than it had been. He hoped to see him in Texas soon.

"I'll get you to the hotel and hopefully make you comfortable." Stetson got in the truck and started to drive.

"I'm the one you've been pining for?" Storm's eyes were wide with pleasure.

"Nope, we were talking about a horse."

"Stetson Scott. If I wasn't in pain I'd sock you one in the shoulder."

He laughed and glanced her way. "You've already given me one black eye. I don't want to be known as a battered husband."

"Oh like that would ever happen."

"I'm a man of the world. I've seen Dr. Phil. I know things, missy."

Storm giggled. "When do you have time to watch talk shows?"

"There's a lot of down time between rodeos. Too much time thinking about regrets."

"We have each other now. Are you going to sit there or are you going to carry me inside the hotel. I was thinking that we could try out that hot tub that's in our room." She gave him a sexy grin and she batted her eyelashes at him.

Stetson didn't bother to answer. He jumped out of the truck and was lifting her out in no time. "Oh, honey, I do love hot tubs."

Storm trailed hot kisses up and down his neck. Stetson would have run to their room given the choice. She was making him crazy. A shiver went through him when she licked the side of his neck. He hoped they didn't run into anyone. He knew his arousal was evident.

"You'll be the death of me," he murmured.

"Mmm, that sounds good, death by tongue." Storm giggled and went back to licking behind his ear.

He fumbled for the room key, trying not to drop her. His legs shook; he needed to sit down. Finally, he got the door open. Rushing in, he gently put her on the bed and plopped down on his back next to her. "You don't play fair."

Storm smiled at him. "What are you talking about?"

Stetson rolled his eyes at her feigned innocence. "Baby, I'm out of my mind right now. I probably don't know what I'm talking about."

"Wasn't there mention of a hot tub?"

"I don't know if it's a good idea. I don't want you to get hurt." The words out of his mouth did not reflect what he felt. He wanted to strip her naked and show her how insane a tongue could make a person.

"Well I'm going in. I'll need your help getting naked." Storm smiled prettily at him.

Stetson groaned and sat up. He framed her beautiful face with his hands. He looked into her eyes hoping she could see the love he held for her. Leaning down, he nipped at her bottom lip. The kiss became full and passion filled. Her lips were so juicy, so smooth, and he couldn't get enough.

He felt her shiver and he pulled back. "Let's get you into the hot tub before I have you flat on your hurt back."

It took everything he had to pull away and she looked as though she was holding in a laugh. "You, my wife, are a first class tease."

"Don't make me beg you to get me naked." Her laughter could no longer be contained. It was a gift to see her so happy, so playful, and so in love.

*****

Storm shivered, waiting for Stetson to help her. She wanted him more than ever. Her ability to tease and arouse him made her feel a confidence she didn't know she had.

He knelt in front of her and took off her shoes. Next, he unbuttoned her jeans and had her lift up so he could strip them from her. Butterflies filled her stomach. He was eye level with her most private of parts. He didn't move, he just stared.

Stetson put his hands on her thighs and she felt such need. He let go of her and stood up.

"Lift your arms." His husky voice made her tingle.

It hurt, but she lifted her arms. Stetson drew her top off and threw it aside. He reached around her and unhooked her pink bra. It fell slowly as she leaned forward.

Storm never wanted anything more than she wanted Stetson. The anticipation alone nearly drove her over the edge. All she wanted was for him to touch her, to make love to her.

He moved closer and Storm quivered. Stetson scooped her up and put her in the bubbling hot tub.

"Oh this feels so good." Closing her eyes, she sighed.

"I'll be back," Stetson called from behind the closing hotel door.

Shocked, she couldn't imagine where he'd gone. The longer she sat there, the madder she got.

The water against her back felt nice and she began to relax. The view out the balcony windows made her glory in the wonder of the majestic Grand Tetons. The tops were white -- snow, she mused. Stetson sure did go all out on the honeymoon suite. It was sheer opulence with gold accents everywhere. The bedspread was adorned with several pillows, all in various shades of gold.

She had laughed last night when she saw the flat

screen television in the bathroom. She had secretly hoped that they would make use of the hot tub. She didn't quite expect to be in it alone though.

She heard the door open and when she looked over, she saw Stetson standing just inside the door holding a bouquet of roses in one hand and a bottle of champagne in the other. The sweetness of it brought tears to her eyes.

"I wanted to do this right." He took three long strides toward her. Bending, he kissed her. "These are for you."

"They look perfect. Red roses, I don't think I ever got roses before."

Stetson smiled and walked over to the wet bar. He opened the champagne with a loud popping of the cork. Filling two flutes, he walked over and handed one to her. "Don't drink it yet, I want to make a toast."

Storm watched as he set his glass down and proceeded to undress. Her stomach quivered when he took off his shirt, exposing his lean, hard muscles. She held her breath watching him remove his pants. She gasped. Her husband was one fine specimen of maleness.

She wanted to gulp down her champagne right then. She shivered in the hot water with desire. "You're not going to leave me in here again, are you?"

Stetson grinned at her, grabbed his glass, and got into the hot tub. "I love you Storm. I have for a very long time. I want to toast to a long and happy marriage." He clinked his glass against hers.

Storm's emotions were on overload. Her body tingled, her heart felt like bursting, and she was on the verge of tears. Sipping the champagne, she felt tears fall onto her face.

Stetson took her glass from her and put it on the edge of the tub. "How does your back feel?"

"A bit better."

He gave her one of his slow sexy smiles and he placed his hands around her waist, lifting her up and over so she was straddling him.

This is what she'd been waiting for, longing for, and she didn't hold back. She took everything he had to give and then some. She didn't want nice and sweet. She just wanted to get down to business. They had the rest of the night for sweet exploration. Before she knew it, she was screaming to the heavens.

Stetson cried out her name and held her tight. "Wow."

"Wow is right."

CHAPTER SIXTEEN

Waking, Storm felt so snuggly warm. Wanting to enjoy the feel of Stetson's brawny arms around her, she stayed still. She knew he wouldn't have her in his arms if awake.

It was going to be a hard day. Stetson may never forgive her, but she was going. Slipping carefully out of the bed, she grabbed her clothes, and took one last glimpse at Stetson.

A smile lingered on her lips while she took in the sight of him, almost boyish in his sleep. His face seemed relaxed, not at all how he appeared when he was awake. Lately he'd looked stressed. It was her hope that going to see her father would take some of the stress away.

She tiptoed down the wooden staircase. Storm concentrated. There were a few steps that creaked, and she needed to avoid them. Relieved with her success, she hurried into the bathroom and got dressed.

After leaving a note next to the coffee pot, she was off. Getting into one of the ranch trucks, she hoped she wouldn't waken anyone when she started the engine. It was still dark out, but she figured the sun would be coming up right about the time she reached her father's ranch.

Her heart beat faster, thinking about the upcoming confrontation. Instinctively, she wanted to turn around and return to the safety of her bed and Stetson's arms. Realistically, she drove on. There would be no real peace until things were resolved.

Her father was a hard man, but she knew he wasn't a killer. Smitty had been his best friend. Storm refused to entertain the idea her father had anything to do with Smitty's death.

Turning onto the dirt road that led to the ranch, she felt sick. Maybe Stetson was right. Maybe she should stay out of it. Taking a deep breath, she drove on. She'd been right, the sun was just rising, and activity had just started on the ranch.

Seeing the log house that she'd grown up in astounded her. She'd missed her home. It looked about the same except there were no flowers anymore. It always amazed her that a house could be made out of massive logs. The porch was the same, but there were no chairs on it.

Before she could fortify herself, the front door swung open and her father bounded out of the house. He swiftly walked over to the truck and opened the door.

Storm didn't know what to expect. She certainly didn't expect her father to pull her into a big bear hug. Returning the hug was impossible. Too much had happened.

"Where is my grandson?" He let her go and looked in the truck.

"It's just me. I need to talk to you." His grandson? What was going on? He'd spent five years denying him.

"You look good, Storm. Come on, let's have some coffee." He led the way inside, grabbed two mugs, and filled them. Motioning for her to sit down, he then handed her one of the mugs.

Storm's heart hurt. Her father looked the same --
big and brawny with thick red hair. The kitchen looked
wonderful. The hand-honed cabinets were pieces of art
that he'd made for her mother. The butcher-block
counters reminded her of happy times spent cooking.

"I'm glad you're here. I suppose you heard about
Smitty?"

Nodding, she took a sip of her coffee. "Stetson
and I found him."

"Oh no, sweetheart. I'm so sorry."

"I'm not your sweetheart anymore, Daddy. I
stopped being your sweetheart the day you threw me off
the ranch."

He mumbled something, and his face grew
bright red. The look of sorrow in his eyes surprised her.
She had long ago thought him to have no feelings. Not
that it mattered now. Sometimes too late really meant too
late. His façade of being contrite was too late.

"Where's Chrissy?" Looking around Storm didn't
spot anything of Chrissy's not even a flip-flop.

"She's taken up with Evers. He's my new
foreman, and since he has a house she skedaddled."

Storm nodded. Nothing surprised her about
Chrissy. "She's not carrying Stetson's child."

"I know." He sat down across from her at the
big oak table. Reaching across, he tried to take her hand.

Storm snatched her hand back quicker than
lightening. "What do you mean you know? For how long
have you known?" Her voice was getting louder, but she
didn't care.

"That there Stamos fellow showed me the
paternity test." At least he managed to look sheepish.

Still, she was unmoved by his sorrow. "Why?"
Storm's heart felt as though it had formed a big lump in
her throat and no other words came out.

"I don't rightly know. Think that little gal is a bit
loco. She had me believing her. I feel like an old fool."

"The Scott's cattle has been rustled. From what I hear, it's been going on for over five years. I found the path in the canyon. I know all about the deals you promised Stetson's dad that would make him money. I know how you bankrupted the whole operation and demanded that Nellie marry you."

She couldn't sit and watch him stare into his coffee anymore. Standing, she took a spot viewing out the window over the kitchen sink. The magnolia trees her father had planted for her mother were thriving. Her mother had been so pleased when they finally bloomed.

"They stole you away from me. It was only fair." The fury in his voice made her shiver.

Turning toward him, she didn't know what to say. Taking a deep breath, she stared him down. "You threw me away like garbage. It had nothing to do with the Scott's."

"You think you know it all. You're stubborn just like your mother. The Scott's started it. I was just finishing it." He shrugged as if it was no big deal.

"I guess it doesn't matter."

"It does matter. They turned me against my own daughter. To my eternal shame, I allowed them to sully your name. I didn't stop them."

Closing her eyes, Storm felt dizzy. Nothing made sense. Not one thing. Cautiously, she walked to the wooden chair and settled herself in it. "I don't know what you're rambling on about."

Her father reached across the table again. He held her hand tightly. It took some pulling, but she snatched it back again. "Don't. Don't touch me!"

His shoulders slumped and he nodded. "I can't say I blame you. That night I went over to the Scotts to make Stetson take responsibility for you and the babe, I was told lies. Lies I'm ashamed to say I believed. Damn, Senior was so convincing. He had two men there to back him and the details they had. It hadn't helped any that

Stetson had fled. It just made their stories of you getting around all the more believable."

Gasping for air, Storm got up and ran outside. She wanted an answer and she got one. Her father thought she was a whore. Pain washed over her. They'd always been so close until that evening. How could he have believed Senior Scott, and not even talk to her about it?

Tears ran down her face. Well, now she knew. Looking in the distance, she saw the dust kicking up on the drive. Someone was in a big hurry.

The screen door slammed and Storm felt her father grab a hold of her arm. It made her cringe. "I'm no good at sayin' sorry."

The tension in her neck and across her shoulders became unbearable. "I don't want or need an apology. Why? Why Chrissy? What was it about her that had you trying to stop my wedding? You would steal away what little happiness I had found and give it to a stranger?" Her chest was heaving, and her heart beat painfully against her ribs.

"You were already branded a whore. I didn't want the same for little Chrissy. She's a sweet little gal. Your reputation had been dragged through the mud so many times."

Staring at him, her heart shattered. She couldn't find the man he used to be. As a child, she thought her father was a loving giant. Now all she saw was a malicious, pathetic, cheat.

The worst part was the way he looked at her as if he expected forgiveness. Shrugging again, he gave her a tentative smile.

Storm's stomach rolled. Spotting the truck flying toward them, she let out half a laugh. Stetson looked none too happy. Storm couldn't face him. Running to her truck, she quickly climbed in, locked the doors, and started the engine.

Making a wide turn, she gunned it down the

drive. Stetson probably wouldn't talk to her now. At least she had a few answers. The truth didn't make her feel one bit better. Her heart squeezed painfully.

"Damn him!" Slamming on the brakes, she hit the steering wheel, hurting her hands. "Damn! Damn!"

Hearing Stetson pulling up behind her, she dreaded the confrontation. *Better here than at the ranch.* There was no need to get others involved.

Taking a deep breath, she exited the truck and looked back at Stetson. She wanted to be brave and stand her ground. She had every right to confront her father. Her mind was ready for battle, but her upset stomach had her running to the other side of the truck, heaving.

*****

Stetson took a deep breath. He wanted to throttle her. Why couldn't she trust him to take care of the situation with her dad? Frankly, it hurt.

Finding her gone this morning provided quite a ride. First, he was worried, then he was angry, and finally he felt as though she cut out a piece of his heart. He didn't know if she'd ever trust him. No trust, no love, that's what he believed.

Pulling his blue bandanna out of his back pocket, he went to her. Her heaving looked painful. He'd been there before. She didn't even give any indication that she knew he was there. Stetson handed her the bandanna and held her waist.

Coughing, Storm shook her head. It was too bad, he wasn't leaving. "I have some water in the truck if you want it?"

"No. No, I can't." Straightening up, her glance found his. The raw pain in her blue eyes was jarring and alarming.

"I wish I could say I'm sorry, but I'm not. I had to find out. I had to know and you not wanting me to talk to him hurt."

Drawing her into his arms, he could feel her tremble. Whatever that son of a bitch said, it was bad. "It's all right. We'll be fine. I'm worried about you though."

She snuggled closer and wrapped her hands around his middle. "I hate him." Tears fell onto his shirt.

"Do you want me to take you home?" He had one hand in her hair and the other rubbed her back. Her trembling began to subside.

"No, let's talk here. I don't want the rest of the family upset."

She said family. Things may be all right, eventually. "Come on, I have an old blanket in the truck and we can sit and watch the leaves change colors."

Storm gave him the slightest smile. "I like to watch the leaves turn." She followed him into the woods.

"A bit chilly, but not too cold." Stetson laid out the old army blanket and waved his hand across it, offering Storm a place to sit.

"Is Nellie watching Scotty?" She sat on the furthest corner of the blanket.

Stetson sat right next to her, giving no quarter. "Joe took him this morning. They are going to Garrett's for a bit."

Storm nodded absently. "I don't know where to begin. I feel as though my life keeps getting shredded and shredded. I can't seem to feel whole. Nothing I do is right. People I trusted betrayed me. I feel as though someone stomped me to the ground and mashed me with the heel of their boot."

Tempted to take her into his arms, he decided to hold off. She didn't look as though she wanted warm and fuzzy at the moment. He yearned to take her pain away. "Why don't you tell me what happened?"

Storm nodded, avoiding his gaze. She picked up a blade of grass and examined it. "Your father convinced my dad that the baby wasn't yours. Senior said I got around and he had two hands there to back him. Oh Stetson, they gave details. My father believed them."

Stetson felt a rage start to run through him. "Did he say which hands claimed to have been with you?"

"No. I didn't think to ask. He gave me a halfhearted sorry as though it would wipe it all away." Storm threw the grass into the air. "I asked about Chrissy. I needed to know why he would defend her when he threw me to the wolves." She hiccupped.

Stetson took her hand. "What did he say?"

Storm finally looked at him. Her forlorn look devastated him. "He said I was already known as a whore, and that I have a bad reputation, and that Chrissy was a sweet little gal."

"That good for nothing--"

Storm shook her head. "It's not worth it. My father conned Senior into bad investments and that's why Nellie was to marry my dad. She was to be a payment so the ranch wouldn't go under."

"Why?"

"He figured out that your father lied about me and wanted revenge I guess. It's all about him. He didn't give a damn about me. So much has happened because of your father's lie." Tears trailed down her cheeks. "Why would he have done such a thing?

"My father was a hard man. I couldn't get along with him." He intertwined his fingers with hers, lifting her hand, and kissed the back of it. "If I hadn't gone off cock sure, none of this would have happened."

"You are not to blame."

He lay down and pulled her on top of him so her ear was over his heart   . "Do you want me to go and sock him one?"

Raising her head, she smiled. "Yes and not just one." She pinned him under her as he made a move to get up. "But don't."

"Why not? He deserves a pounding."

Putting her fingers over his lips, she smiled. "It's enough that you want to pound him. Stetson, I'm sorry. I should have talked things out with you instead of flying over to my dad's. I should have trusted you. I'm not saying you were right and I was wrong, but I shouldn't have worried you."

Stetson smiled back at her. "As long as we have each other, we can move mountains."

"Mountains?"

Stetson looked down her shirt. "Yes, two very fine mountains."

Storm stared at him and laughed. "My heart still feels like it's been ripped apart, but being with you makes it easier. I prefer to think of them as nicely rounded hills."

Rolling so that Storm was under him, he looked into her eyes. The love he felt was all in that one look. Leaning down, he kissed her. "I love you."

"I know."

"If it were any other day I'd strip your clothes off and make sweet love to you."

Storm shivered. "Today sounds good."

"No honey, your feelings are too raw. I want to make love to you and know that you trust me enough to be included in your life."

"I—"

Stetson shook his head. "I'll hold you, I'll bathe you, and I'll sing to you to make you happy and to help you forget your father. I will not be your panacea." He kissed her again, this time he stroked her cheek. "Do you know what I'm saying?"

"I do actually. I don't want to have regrets later, but it sure as hell would have been fun."

Storm stood and Stetson watched her walk to her truck with misgivings. Had he done the wrong thing by refusing to make love with her? She seemed to understand, but the pain in her eyes ate at him.

Maybe he was just trying to be noble, not

Kathleen Ball

realistic. Damn it, his wife needed comfort and he offered a bath. When he made the offer, he'd been sincere. He grabbed the blanket and walked to his truck, watching the dust kick into the air from the truck Storm drove. Punching the truck door, he stared at it. Damn it, that was his wife suffering. Her world had come down on her today and he failed her.

Shaking his head as he drove home, he recognized the ridiculousness of the whole thing. He'd been thinking of nothing but getting into bed with Storm. Calling himself a clueless cowboy, he got out of the truck. Doubt assailed him. What if she didn't want to make love after his speech?

Taking off his Stetson, he raked his fingers through his curly blond hair. He almost laughed. What the hell was he doing outside? Storm needed him and he'd oblige her any way she wanted. Yep, rocks for a brain, that's what he had.

His time for thinking was cut short. Buck came bounding out of the house along with Scotty. Stetson picked up Scotty and held him close.

"Hey partner, why all the tears?"

"Nellie said that Mommy was phroke-ed. She barely said hi to me and she didn't say hi to Buck. Can we fix her?"

Stetson's heart ached. While he'd been thinking about sex, his son thought Storm was broken. "Let's go into the house and see what we can do."

Scotty nodded his head against Stetson's shoulder. "I'm a good fixer, Daddy."

"I know, cowboy."

Nellie looked worried. She held out her arms to take Scotty, but he had a death grip around Stetson's neck. Nodding at Stetson, she backed off.

"So tell me, cowboy, what would make you feel better if you were sad?" Stetson asked him.

Loosening his grip, Scotty looked solemnly into

Stetson's eyes. "Cookies and milk."

Feeling his lips begin to twitch, he kissed his son's forehead. "Sounds like a good plan."

Putting Scotty down, he grabbed an old wooden tray and three plastic cups. Filling them with milk, he hoped that Scotty's plan worked, a bit. "Grab the cookies for me."

Scotty grabbed a chair, pushed it over to the counter, and climbed onto it. He grabbed a plate, and carefully put it down. Opening the cookie jar, he took out handfuls of chocolate chip cookies that his Aunt Nellie had made. "How's that, Daddy?"

"Looks good, champ." Stetson took the cookie-laden plate and added it the milk on the tray. "Let's go cheer up your mother."

Scotty ran up the stairs ahead of Stetson, but he waited at the door for him. Stetson nodded and Scotty opened the door.

"Your guys are here, Mommy!"

Scotty's face was bright and smiling in stark contrast to Storm's red and pain filled face. Stetson's heart turned over when he saw his wife trying to smile. She certainly was a trooper.

"I'm so glad you're here. I was feeling a bit blue, but I'm better now that you're here." Her try at cheerfulness amazed him.

"Scotty suggested cookies and milk for sad times. I agree." Setting the tray on the table, he handed out the cups of milk. Winking at Storm, he put the plate of cookies on her lap.

Scotty sat on one side of her and Stetson sat on the other side. Kissing her neck, he smiled. "Feeling better?"

She nodded and gave them both a tremulous smile. "How could I not feel better? I have my guys and the special milk and cookies treatment. I'm blessed and pleased to have you both."

"You betcha! You are the luckiest mommy in the whole world and when my brother or sister comes I'll be the happiest brother!"

Wide-eyed, Stetson turned and stared at Storm. The look of confusion on her face mirrored his. "Maybe someday partner, but not right now."

Scotty nodded his head. "Yep, Aunt Nellie told me so."

"What did she say exactly, kiddo?" Storm handed him another cookie.

"That you were sick a lot and you had all the signs. I've looked, but I don't see any signs."

Storm looked at Stetson. "Do you know what he's talking about?"

"Scotty, when did Aunt Nellie tell you this?" Stetson felt his heart beat faster.

Scotty frowned. "I know'd that I wasn't apposed to hear, but Aunt Nellie told Joe. They kept saying it's a secret."

Storm laughed a deep, hearty laugh. She kissed Scotty's head and reached for Stetson's hand. Placing it on her abdomen, she laughed again. "Now that I think about it, I think she's right."

Nellie's head poked in, her eyes twinkling with excitement. "I couldn't help but overhear."

Storm shook her head. "How?"

"You've been running to the restroom pretty regularly now." Nellie laughed and held out her hand to Scotty. "Come on, cow-poke. I'll finish reading the book we started."

Scotty jumped out of bed and raced out of the room.

"Must be some book." Stetson cocked one eyebrow.

"Oh it is. It's about cowboys. You two enjoy." Nellie closed the door behind her.

"I don't know if I should laugh or cry. We never

talked about having more children and I was leaning toward leaving and... Children are a blessing, of course I want more." He put his arms around her, pulling her head to his chest.

"It's the middle of the day and here we are in bed. I need to get up and give Nellie a hand around the house."

Stetson laughed. "I'm sure it's fine." Pulling back, he grew serious. "We have a few things to talk about, my sweet."

Sighing, Storm nodded. "I always seem to be doing the wrong thing. Of course you didn't want to make love to me. I feel disgusted with myself for wanting it."

Stetson brushed her hair back from her face. "You are a very complex woman. My woman. Don't feel disgusted. I was the one at fault. Who am I to dictate what type of comfort you should have. I was being an ass, but in my defense I thought it was the noble thing to do."

"Noble hurts my heart. No more noble."

Stetson heart twisted at the pain he saw in her blue eyes. "I can't promise not to be noble, it's in my DNA. I will however promise to think before I open my big mouth."

Giving him a ghost of a smile, she seemed at a loss as to what to say.

"I don't know what to do now. I want to be your comfort, but I don't want to cross any lines or create any more hurts." He held his breath waiting for her response.

"I feel like I'm jumping out of my skin. I'm hurt and upset and exhilarated all at the same time." Putting her head on his shoulder, she sighed.

"I can't believe we're having a baby." He felt his eyes tear up. "I missed everything while you were pregnant with Scotty. I can't wait to be a part of this pregnancy."

Storm stretched up and kissed his eyelids. "The joy outweighs the misery. I'm not going to think about my father anymore today. I do know what I want though."

Her sultry voice washed over him, making him instantly hard. "Oh yeah? What might that be?"

"I want to have my way with you, cowboy." Straddling him, she leaned down and kissed him.

Her lips felt so soft, and he groaned as she put her tongue in his mouth. She tasted like everything wonderful, but most of all she tasted like chocolate chip cookies. "Mm my favorite."

"What?" She breathed the word into his mouth.

"You taste so good." Stetson grabbed her waist, intending to lay her under him, but she put her hands over his and shook her head.

"I can't have my way with you if I'm on the bottom now can I?"

Stetson's hands stilled and his heart beat faster. "What are we talking about here?"

Reaching down, she pulled the hem of her shirt up and over her head.

The black lace bra she wore hid nothing. "Where'd you get that?"

Smiling, she reached behind her and unhooked it, letting it fall off her breasts. "Nellie took me shopping."

She unbuttoned his shirt, and began to kiss him up and down his chest. When she got to his jeans she unbuttoned them, continuing in her exploration of his body.

It became obvious that having her way meant that she was going to torture him. All he wanted was to see if she had matching black panties and take them off her. "If you don't stop that I'm going to explode."

She gave him a wicked grin. "Am I too much for you?"

"Hell yes!"

Storm stood up and unsnapped her jeans, pushing them down. She was indeed wearing matching black lace panties. They didn't hide much either. She turned around and he gulped. It was a thong.

"Oh God, are you sexy. Get that pretty little ass over here. I have needs you know."

Storm laughed and stripped off her thong. Climbing on top of him, she smiled.

He growled loudly as he exploded. He watched as she flung her head back and moaned his name, shuddering in his arms. She put her head on his shoulder.

"I think I like this having my way thing."

"I like my way too." Stetson held her and turned them so that he was on top. He couldn't believe he still had enough energy, but he had to have her again.

Finally satiated, they fell asleep.

CHAPTER SEVENTEEN

The next day, Storm felt less troubled. Watching Stetson, Scotty, and Buck all romp around the yard kept her smiling. She'd just have to get over her hurts. The past was the past. More cattle were missing, not many, but enough to make Stetson livid.

Holding herself around the middle, she felt at peace. A baby, imagine that. What would it be like to have love and support this time around? Storm had high hopes.

Dust was rising on the dirt road. Stepping outside, she had to shield her eyes from the blazing sun with her hand. It looked like Joe's truck. Something was wrong, he wasn't a fast driver.

Stetson noticed too. He carried Scotty to the front porch and stood beside her.

The door behind her squeaked as it opened and soon Nellie was at her other side. "I wonder what's wrong?" Her voice quavered, prompting Storm to put her arm around her.

The truck came to a skidding stop and Joe practically flew out the door. "McCrory's been arrested for Smitty's death."

"No, it can be." Storm's heart seemed to have stopped.

"Well hell. I don't like the man, but he's no killer." Stetson handed Scotty to Storm. "I need to make a few calls."

"Daddy said hell. You're not supposed to say hell." Scotty looked very serious.

"You are right, kiddo. No dessert for him tonight." Storm ruffled his blond curls and put him down. He was off like a shot with Buck at his feet.

Joe kissed Nellie. "You two mamas need to get off your feet."

"Not until—" Storm started.

"Just sit and I'll tell you what I know. You sure are stubborn, Storm Scott."

Both women sat on the wooden porch chairs, looking expectantly at Joe. "Seems they have a witness. That Sam Evers, his new foreman, says he saw the whole thing. Never did like that Evers. No good if you ask me."

"If Evers said it, then it's not true. He was one of the first to say that he might be Scotty's father. He harassed me to no end. Why though? I just don't understand."

The screen door opened again and Stetson joined them, leaning against the porch railing. "I have an idea why. Evers has been our main suspect in the cattle rustling. I sat down with Garrett and Stamos the other day with all my father's files, and while it is true that McCrory basically bled him dry, there still are a lot of cattle unaccounted for."

"Stetson, Chrissy is with Sam. She can't be safe with him." Storm bit her lip in worry.

Stetson ran his fingers through his hair. "She's been fine so far. She's not my main concern. You are."

Storm gasped. "Why me? I'm perfectly fine."

"Now this is all rumor and Joe can back me on that." Joe nodded. "Your father put Evers in his will in the case of his and your death."

"Who would be so stupid?" Nellie asked.

"It sounds like some sort of blackmail." Joe stood up. "I've got to go figure out how we lost that cattle. They didn't use the canyon; I have that place guarded. Let me know if you hear anything." He pulled Nellie up into his arms and kissed her. He hung on to her for a moment before he let her go. "Love you."

"Love you too."

Storm scooted to the edge of her chair. "Okay, what's the plan?"

"Plan? Oh no, you are not getting involved. I don't want either of you doing one damned thing."

"No dessert for two nights," Scotty called.

Storm's lips twitched. "You swore twice."

Stetson grinned. "Darn, I like dessert. I'm going into town to talk to your father, alone."

Storm knew when she was beat. Besides, she could wait for Stetson to leave and she and Nellie could come up with a plan. Maybe she'd call Callie and Joy.

*****

Joy shook her head. She placed her teacup down on the kitchen table. "I'm all for finding out the truth, but never quote me on this: maybe the men are right."

Callie brushed a piece of blonde hair out of her eyes. "What the heck? Joy, have you gone all girly on me? Come on, we're strong intelligent women, surely we can figure out what Sam Evers is up to."

Joy glanced at Callie then at Storm. Finally her gaze rested on Nellie. "I just want to be sure that we don't get hurt. Nellie looks like she's about to pop."

Nellie blushed. "I'm not due for three more months. Besides, Storm is now my sister and I want to help."

Storm smiled at them. She felt blessed to have

such good friends. She knew how lonely life could be without anyone to talk to, anyone to count on. "I'm not proposing we take any action. Well, at least not yet. Maybe Callie could happen to befriend Chrissy or something. We need more info."

"Ha! That's the spirit!" Callie gave Joy an 'I told you so' look. "I'm on it. I have to tell you, it's an assignment I'm not looking forward to. She's loco."

Storm stood up and paced the kitchen a few times. She'd felt as though her past, her father, would never be behind her. "Don't take any chances, but maybe we could each find out what the men are up to. You know as well as I they are planning something. We need the skinny on Sam. He has some hold over my father and I'd like to know what it is. Stetson said Sam won't be happy until both my father and I are dead. That's not happening."

Joy jumped up and gave Storm a quick hug. "I'm in. Don't you worry, we'll get this all figured out."

Storm smiled warmly at her friend. "Thanks, I appreciate it."

She knew he was there before he even spoke. She could feel his warm breath on the back of her neck. She hoped he didn't hear much.

"What's all the thanks for?" He tipped his hat. "Ladies, nice to see you. Did my wife happen to mention she's pregnant?"

Callie smiled at him. "Of course she told us, that's what the thanks are for. Between Joy and me, we have a mountain of baby clothes for both her and Nellie."

Storm was so glad that she wasn't facing her husband at the moment. The corners of her mouth curved upward as though she wanted to laugh.

Callie stood and stepped on Storm's foot. That made her stop smiling. "Well I guess we should get back to our roosts."

"Thank you both for inviting us to tea." Joy kissed both Nellie and Storm on the cheek.

"I'll call with the info on the baby things." Callie waved as she followed Joy out the door.

Storm turned and studied Stetson. Either he knew what they were up to or he had his own secret. Too afraid to ask, she went to him and kissed his whiskered cheek. "You are too handsome for your own good."

Grinning widely, he took her into his arms and hugged her. "Better be about baby things," he whispered.

"You worry too much. What happened in town? How's my father? Oh God, I can't believe I even care, but I do."

"That's because you have a big heart," Nellie said, right before she left the room.

Storm rubbed herself against Stetson. She could feel every hard tight plane of his body. "We're alone in the kitchen."

"True."

"You haven't ever wanted to have sex in the kitchen?"

Shaking his head he looked at her adoringly. "Right now I'm thinking about it, but since we don't live alone it wouldn't be a good idea. Besides, I'm on to you. You just want to distract me with that delectable body of yours."

Putting her hand over her mouth to stem her laughter didn't help. Finally she looked at him. "Did it work?"

*****

The next day, Nellie and Storm toiled in the fall vegetable garden. They wanted to get it done early in the day before it got too warm. The pumpkins were starting to turn from green to a deep orange.

"I don't know why you insisted on coming out here." Storm glanced at Nellie. "You should be taking it easy."

"I'm pregnant, not sick. Besides, I like gardening, don't you?"

She thought about lying but why bother? "No, I don't like worms."

Nellie laughed. "You spend more than half your life outside; surely you know worms won't hurt you."

"I don't care. They are slimy creatures that pop up from the dirt when you least expect it."

The sound of hooves riding hard stole their attention. Storm watched Nellie put her hands on her lower back and stretch. Joe's horse was easy enough to recognize, but Joe wasn't riding it.

"What in the world. Who is that?" Nellie grabbed Storm's hand, squeezing it tight. "Where do you suppose Joe is?"

Storm put her arm around Nellie's trembling body. "It's Benji from Stamos and Joy's place."

Benji was known as the gentle giant. He'd been hit in the head by a prison guard and ended up mentally impaired.

"Miss Nellie! There's been trouble. Joe sent me. Told me to say that you are not to worry and..." Benji scrunched up his face as though he was trying to think. "He wants you all to be ready when Mr. Garrett comes to get you."

Storm's hand was now being squeezed painfully. "Benji, get down and tell us what happened."

Benji swung down from Joe's horse. If she hadn't already known that he was a big teddy bear, she'd be frightened. Benji was a massive man.

"Miss Myrtle, she all dead now. Mr. Garrett will keep you safe."

Storm gasped. She'd known Myrtle all her life. She'd been like a mother to her, except for when she'd been kicked out of the house. When they'd see each other in town, Myrtle would give her a look of longing and then turn away. It had hurt. It just reinforced that she was a throw away person.

Nellie let go of Storm and grabbed Benji's arm. "Joe is all right?"

"Of course he is. He sent me. Let me ride his horse and everything!" Benji flashed a big smile.

Storm grabbed her cellphone from her pocket and hit speed dial. It rang a few times and then went to voicemail. Of all times, she hung up without leaving a message.

Garrett's truck could be seen in the distance. Storm wondered what happened. She prayed fervently that Myrtle died in her sleep, but her gut told her she hadn't.

Garrett parked in front of the farmhouse. Getting out, he put a smile on his face. It was easy enough for Storm to see past the smile to the worry he harbored.

"Good job, Benji. Where's the munchkin?"

"Scotty is napping." The slamming of the screen door and robust barking soon disputed her claim.

Garrett crouched down until he was at eye level with Scotty. "I'm here to take you to my house for a bit."

"Yeah! Can Buck come too?"

"You bettcha. Nellie, I need you to come with me too."

Storm was surprised. "Not me?"

"Would you come?"

"No."

"Stetson told me you'd refuse. He'll be here in a few." His gaze locked with hers. He looked upset.

Storm longed to question him, but didn't. She didn't want Scotty to know something was wrong. Instead she picked up her young son and put him in the truck with Buck at his side. Kissing him, she hoped all would be fine.

"You be a good boy and have a ton of fun."

"Bye, Mommy." He giggled as Storm kissed his neck.

Storm and Nellie exchanged worried glances and gave each other encouraging smiles. She stood in the yard waving. Storm's heart tightened excruciatingly, and she felt as though she couldn't quite catch her breath.

Running inside, she headed straight for the gun safe in Stetson's office. Luckily she knew the combination. She opened it, grabbed a rifle, and checked to see if it was loaded. Grabbing more ammo, she shoved her jeans pockets full.

Now it was time to wait. Storm went out the front door, and sat down on one of the wooden porch chairs. Her hands trembled as she thought of the possibilities. Damn Sam Evers! He probably killed Smitty. What had happened to Myrtle?

Slowing her breathing, she tried to calm herself. She wouldn't be able to shoot sam full of holes if her hands were shaking.

CHAPTER EIGHTEEN

Staring down the drive, Storm finally calmed herself. The not knowing what happened to Myrtle scared her. She tried to call Stetson, but all she got was his voicemail. What in the world could be going on? Damn her stubborn hide! She wished she'd gone with Scotty and Nellie.

She needed to change her thinking. Somehow she equated needing or accepting help with weakness. She was standing in her own way. It was a necessary way to be when she was alone and vulnerable, but she was married now. She had Stetson, and many friends.

So lost in thought, she failed to hear an approaching horse until an arrow just missed her head. She ducked and dropped to the ground. She could still feel the swoosh of air on her cheek that the arrow had made before it became embedded into the house.

Now she heard the sound of a horse galloping away. Still, she waited on the porch floor. Just because the horse left didn't mean the rider left too.

Saying a quick prayer, she slowly rose up enough to barely see over the bushes, her rifle at hand. Her heart beat so hard she could hear its echo. Scanning the yard, she failed to locate anyone. Staying low, she slowly made her way inside.

With rifle in hand, she checked the doors and windows. She pulled a chair into the hallway that led from the front door to the back door in the kitchen. She'd be able to guard both doors at once.

She refused to think about how close that had been. She needed her thoughts on survival. She had so much to live for, especially Scotty and the baby.

The waiting became unbearable. Finally, she heard a truck pull into the drive. She didn't dare leave her post to see who it was. She'd have to wait until they were at the door. She took a deep breath and bit her bottom lip. *Please, please let it be Stetson.*

*****

Opening the front door, Stetson was shocked when he was greeting by the barrel of a rifle. He immediately grabbed it, and aimed it at the ceiling instead of him.

Storm looked awfully white. Her eyes were wide open, and she appeared terrified. "I'm glad you're all right."

Storm nodded, handing him the rifle. Shaking like a rattlesnake's tail, she just stared at him. She clasped her hands together, took a deep breath, and sighed.

"You're here."

"Storm, what can you tell me about the arrow stuck into the wall at front of the house?"

Storm looked a bit dazed. "I'm too stubborn. I should have gone with Garrett. I almost got killed. The arrow missed me by inches."

"Son of a bitch! Let's go into the family room and talk. You don't look so good."

Grabbing his sleeve, Storm turned her frightened eyes on him. "I want out. I can't stay here. Whoever it was might be back."

"All the more reason to stay put. I don't want to be attacked trying to get to the truck."

Storm nodded and let go of his sleeve. "Scotty?"

"Fine. He's fine." Taking her hand, he gently led her to the brown leather couch. He let her settle in then he sat next to her.

"Myrtle is dead, Stetson. Someone killed her."

"I know honey. I found her this morning."

"What happened?"

Stetson hesitated. He didn't want her any more upset than she already was. On the other hand, she deserved the truth.

"I know it must have been bad. Just tell me."

Stetson took his hat off and threw it onto the coffee table. "The coroner thinks she was strangled first."

Storm gasped. "First?"

"Apparently she was tied to the back of some vehicle and dragged a good many miles."

"Oh, my God. Oh, poor Myrtle. I hope she was already dead before they, they..." Tears poured down her face. She looked so hopeless that it broke his heart.

"I made some headway with the prosecutor. He doesn't think your father is guilty, but in light of the new murder, we all agreed that Pat would be better off in his cell, safer."

"Myrtle never hurt anyone. Smitty neither. It seems like I'm watching some insane movie. Did they arrest Sam Evers?"

"Not enough evidence, yet. You and Scotty are both in danger. I want to send Scotty to an FBI friend of Stamos' for a few days. She's supposed to be very good."

"You're going to send my baby away?" She hiccupped as she cried louder.

Getting off the couch, Stetson knelt in front of her, taking her hands in his. He could feel her shaking. "We need him safe and Janey is the police chief's niece. Stamos has worked with her."

She studied his face and finally nodded.

"Storm, why didn't you call for help?"

She looked puzzled, then amazed. "I have no idea. I was waiting for you and then the arrow-- I suppose I went into survival mode and didn't think of it."

"It's all right, honey. We're safe, that's all that counts."

"What about Chrissy? Is she still with Evers?"

Stetson shrugged his shoulder. "No one seems to have seen her."

*****

It seemed as though the police were taking their sweet time looking at the arrow and speculating. Storm knew that the Lasso Springs police force was small. If they were all here staring at the damn arrow, who was trying to find the shooter?

Sitting at the kitchen table, she couldn't take it anymore. Standing up, she sent her chair flying backwards. Storm stomped out of the house, slamming the door behind her.

The tension in her body grew unbearable. The muscles in her neck and shoulders were so tight it grew painful. Even her face felt pinched. She could only imagine it wasn't her best look.

Blackmail sounded like the best theory. What did Evers have on her father? She had no idea. She'd been disowned, she thought bitterly. Smitty probably knew and it cost him his life. Did Myrtle know too? How can anyone treat a woman so despicably?

Dead was dead, why drag her body around? Was it a message to her father to keep his mouth shut? The whole will thing made no sense.

Sighing, she realized she didn't have one answer. Information was power and right now she felt as helpless as a new born chick.

Hearing the door behind her open and close, she assumed that Stetson was behind her. "I can't take being cooped up any longer."

"You'd better get used to it."

Storm whirled around and found herself face to face with Stamos Walker.

"Look, Storm, I know how you feel, but standing out here making a target of yourself is not helping. Get in the house."

His voice was calm and steady. Storm could tell he was serious. Nodding, she walked in front of him and back into the kitchen. "I just wish we knew what we're up against."

Her cheeks grew wet as her tears trailed down them. Stamos quickly took her into his arms and held her.

"I can take it from here." Stetson took her hand and drew her close.

"I was just trying to help."

"No problem, Stamos. I'm glad you're here." Stetson looked down at her. "And you my dear wife, no more wandering."

In any other situation she'd probably argue with his high handedness. She realized he was right. "I'm sorry. I wasn't thinking."

Stetson cradled her against his body. He rubbed his hands up and down her back. Pulling away, he looked at her face. The love in his eyes gave her strength.

Leaning down, Stetson nibbled on her bottom lip before he possessed her with his mouth. He thrust his tongue in her mouth and danced with her tongue. He pulled her closer and she could feel his need.

The kiss went on making her head spin. How she loved this man!

"Hey kids, let's get all our facts laid out. Maybe there's something we missed." Chief Gordon smiled at them.

Reluctantly, Storm stepped away. Her lips felt electrified and her body hummed. Chief Gordon was right. They needed to talk about the facts.

Kathleen Ball

CHAPTER NINETEEN

Mucking hay was just the type of work Storm needed. The physical exertion helped her to keep her sanity. Going over the facts with Chief Gordon hadn't really told her anything new.

The state police had been called in to help and they were in town strategizing with the chief. They already had permission from her father to search the ranch and they were busy making plans. Plans she was not privy to.

Stetson was busy with the horses, but she knew that he was keeping an eye on her. Feeling protected was a mixed blessing. The gratefulness she felt was dusted with the frustration of being constantly observed.

She missed Scotty the most. She didn't dare go to Garrett's. There was the fear she'd lead Evers right to him and Storm would do anything to keep her son safe.

She kept going, working and working nonstop until finally she felt Stetson's hand on her shoulder. He looked tired and concerned.

"That's enough for one day. It'll be getting dark soon." He took the shovel from her and leaned it against the stall.

"I lost track of the time."

"I would have asked you to stop hours ago, but I could see the hard work was cathartic. I do the same thing. Sometimes it gets rid of my anger and sometimes I end up with the answer to my problem"

Storm leaned into him. The smell of horses was on him and she loved it. Stepping in front of him, she wrapped her arms around his trim waist, and put her cheek on his muscular chest.

Stetson held her back, and it brought tears to her eyes. Right now she liked being protected.

The ringing of Stetson's phone drew them apart. Storm watched his face anxiously for any clues.

"They made the raid. Evers is in jail along with one of the hands. Does the name Blue Sawyer mean anything to you?"

Storm shook her head.

"I guess that's who helped him. They found enough evidence to put him away for a long time."

Breathing a sigh of relief, Storm tried to smile, but it really wasn't a time to smile. "What about Chrissy?"

"They believe she's with her brother. They are trying to get ahold of him now."

"Even though she was a big pain, I'm glad she wasn't hurt." Storm took Stetson's hand and squeezed it. "I know you were friends for a long time."

"Hopefully, Brian will be able to straighten her out."

"We can get back to normal."

Stetson gave her a long look. "What is normal to you? I want to start out on the right foot."

Stetson sat on a bale of hay. He reached up and pulled her down next to him. He wanted his answer; it was evident in his intense perusal.

Storm shifted her body trying to get comfortable on the hay. She was also stalling. What did he want her to say? What if he didn't feel the same way? He came back and in truth, he married her because of Scotty. Did he really love her? Trusting and believing came hard to her. Was he acting like he loved her because of the baby? Doubts, her life had been full of them. Truth be told, she didn't know what normal was anymore.

"This is what I know. I know you are a good husband. I know you love Scotty to bits and you are so good with him. I know you're excited about the new baby. I know you'll always look out for me. I know if you leave I'll be provided for."

She felt Stetson stiffen. "I'm not done. I know you are a fine, honorable man. You are strong when you need to be, but you are also gentle. I also know that if your father hadn't died, you wouldn't have come back. I know you love the rodeo; I don't blame you. Perhaps Chrissy just wanted and needed you. In a way, you left her too. At least in her mind."

Glancing at Stetson, she could see that he was having a hard time keeping quiet. Her heart felt as though it had gone through a wheat thresher. It felt all kinds of shredded. Should she mention love? It just might complicate everything. If he didn't love her back, really love her, she knew she'd break inside.

Was she strong enough to know the truth? She'd had to be strong for some time now, but this was different. Storm felt so raw, so vulnerable. She wanted to tell him that her love was a forever kind of love, but she couldn't take that chance.

*****

Stetson was quiet for a while. He knew what he wanted, but he wasn't sure that it would come out right. He was afraid of saying the wrong thing and sending her running.

"You're probably right about my coming back. I hadn't planned on it, but damn it, Storm, I'm so glad I did. Not because you needed me. Not because of Scotty -- well, he was an extra bonus. I'm forever grateful that I came back and found my heart and soul again. Darlin', parts of them have been missing since I left you. Yes I'm excited about the new baby and I want us to be a family. I want to take care of you and protect you."

Stoking her cheek, he turned her head so she was facing him. "You forgot one thing, Storm Scott. I love you. I know now I always have and I always will. You make me feel like I want to be a better man. You make me feel whole again."

Tears ran down her face and he wiped them away with his thumbs. "I love you." He placed his lips tenderly over hers, giving her short little kisses. He licked her lips and she opened for him. Stetson deepened the kiss until he could feel it in his toes. This was one filly that wasn't going to get away.

Cradling her face in his hands, he kissed her eyelids. "We're both stubborn, but that doesn't matter. If we just talk to each other, we can work out anything. I love you and the whole package; Scotty and the new baby."

Storm flung her arms around his neck and held him close. "I love you too, Stetson. I love you so much it frightens me."

Stetson stroked her back and bent to her ear. "I'm not going anywhere and that's a promise."

Storm nodded and buried her face in his neck. Finally, her tears stopped and they just sat on the bale of hay holding each other.

Stetson never wanted to let her go. It felt too right to have her in his arms. He regretted ever leaving, but what was done was done. He felt lucky to have Storm as his wife and the mother of his children. Things could have turned out so differently and he was blessed.

CHAPTER TWENTY

Watching Scotty trying to play with Buck and not get dirty made her smile. Finally, there was an occasion for smiles. She'd already been to two funerals this past week. Nellie and Joe's wedding would be just the event to put everything back to rights.

Smoothing her hands down the feathery layers of her bridesmaid dress she realized that when all else fails, you just gotta laugh. A big yellow canary, that's what she looked like. She just didn't have the heart to tell Nellie that she didn't want to wear the bird dress. Nellie loved the dress.

Familiar footsteps behind her made her tingle. Stetson put his arms around her middle and pulled her back against him. He kissed the side of her neck and she shivered.

"You are one sexy duck."

"Duck?" Storm turned in his arms. "I'm a canary. I'm surprised you don't know your birds." Laughing, she reached up and fixed his bowtie. "You make a very handsome penguin."

Stetson leaned down and kissed her lips. Each kiss was like the first, exciting and filled with promises. She felt so warm and bubbly inside.

"Yuck! Yuck! Yuck!"

Taking a step back, she had to bite her bottom lip to keep from laughing. "Don't my two men look handsome."

Scotty pulled at his bowtie. "If this is handsome, I'd rather look like a horse's ass."

Storm's mouth dropped open. "Young man--"

Stetson touched her arm. "It's my fault. We were getting dressed, and well, I guess I said it."

Looking from one to the other, she couldn't decide who looked guiltier. Scotty's eyes were open wide, and he kept looking away. Stetson's face had turned bright red and he seemed speechless.

Grabbing their hands, she led them outside. "No cussing at the wedding."

"Yeah, Daddy. Don't get me in any more trouble."

Stetson stopped and lifted Scotty in his arms. "I'll try. Let's go get Aunt Nellie and Uncle Joe hitched."

The ceremony was held in the yard under an arch of yellow roses. Nellie glowed in her simple white dress. Her bouquet was made up of red roses while Storm's was yellow roses.

Joe looked awfully nervous, the 'I'm going to faint' type of nervous, but he prevailed.

Storm looked at Stetson. The love in his eyes humbled her. Feeling her eyes start to pool, she wished the tears back, but a few escaped.

After the minister said, "You may kiss the bride", Storm heard a whispered yuck. Stetson's lips twitched as he put his hand on Scotty's shoulder and pulled him closer. Storm had to look away. Her emotions were going crazy. She wanted to laugh and cry all at the same time. Hormones, she mused.

The wedding was small and intimate. Callie, Garrett, Joy, and Stamos were all there, as were all the men that worked on the ranch. Storm just hoped the time for smiles lasted.

*****

Bustling around the kitchen, Storm began to hum. It struck her that she hadn't sung in a very long while. She hoped Nellie and Joe were having great time in Dallas. They'd planned on only going for a few days, but Stetson paid for the honeymoon suite for a week.

On the kitchen table were the plans for a new house. Storm was glad she insisted Nellie have the choice of houses. Nellie didn't pick the new one. She loved the house she was raised in.

The construction of the new house would be starting any day. Hearing tiny footsteps from upstairs, Storm rolled up the plans and set them aside.

Scotty went racing by and opened the door. "It's an emergency, Mommy. Buck really has to go." Scotty raced for the bathroom himself.

Her heart grew warm. She loved and was loved.

"Cute as a doodlebug on a summer's morn." Stetson stood at the doorway, a teasing glint was in his eyes.

"Why thank you."

"I meant Scotty." Stetson ducked as the dishtowel went flying near his head. He took two long strides and came toe to toe with her. Grabbing her waist, he lifted her up for a quick kiss then let her slide down the length of his chiseled body.

"You are a beautiful sunflower swaying in the wind."

Storm smiled. "That beats doodlebug by a mile. Sit down, I have breakfast almost finished."

"I thought the smell of coffee and eggs made you sick."

"Not this morning for some reason. I feel really

227

good."

Storm opened the door for Buck and she saw a truck coming up the drive. "Looks like we have company."

Stetson was at her side in a flash. "It's Stamos."

"Oh. Did you two have plans to meet?"

Stetson shook his head. Storm didn't like the worried look in his eyes.

*****

Stetson stepped outside. He didn't want to have Storm or Scotty upset if it was bad news. As Stamos walked toward the house, Stetson walked out to greet him.

"I have some news."

"Figured as much."

Stamos' face looked grim. "McCrory's barn was burned down last night. Surprised you didn't hear all the fire trucks."

Stetson could feel himself blush. "I, us, we well-- We were busy."

"Understandable then." Stamos grinned.

"Do they know who did it?"

"Not a clue. With Evers and Blue Sawyer locked up, I thought the trouble was over. Guess someone still has it out for McCrory. Storm and Scotty might not be safe."

Stetson ran his hand over his face. "We need to figure this out and fast. I can't have them in danger. What did McCrory say?"

"He seemed puzzled about the whole thing."

"Thanks for driving out here and letting me know."

"Garrett and I want you to join us at McCrory's around ten o'clock. I'd like to personally question him. He hasn't told the whole truth."

"I'll be there." They shook hands and Stetson watched Stamos leave. He knew he had to go back inside, but he hated to worry Storm."

Taking a deep breath he walked inside and sat at the table. "This looks good."

Storm stood by the stove, staring at him. "Well?"

Stetson quickly glanced at his son. "Well, it seems like your father's barn got a bit damaged." He cringed at the look of alarm on Storm's face.

"Anything we can do?" Her face looked drawn.

"Nope. Sit and eat, we can talk later. I have some work I have to get to and then I have a meeting."

Storm nodded and sat down. He noticed that she barely touched her food. She didn't need more worries. She'd been through enough.

Trust had been a real issue for Storm. He decided to tell her everything. No sugar coating the danger. Damn, he really thought the trouble was over.

*****

Storm waited all morning for an explanation, but there was a problem with one of the horses and Stetson left without telling her a thing. Speculation was driving her mad. She saw him run from the barn and hop into his truck. He was probably going to his meeting.

All she knew was that she was to stay inside with the windows and doors locked. Her nerves felt raw. Trying to keep Scotty entertained until naptime had been a chore. He was used to wide open spaces now and being cooped up made him cranky.

Even Buck seemed to be unhappy with her. He gave her a couple not so nice looks and walked away.

What or who damaged her father's barn? Well, it was probably who. He still had enemies she supposed and that meant she had to be on her guard. Plopping down on the couch, she leaned her head back. Exhaustion filled her whole body. Her eyes closed.

A noise on the porch had her sitting up and

anxious. She could see a shadow outside of the window. Damn, she wished she had the rifle with her, but with Scotty around...

The screen door creaked and the door handle jiggled. Storm raced into action. Running to the fireplace, she tried to reach the rifle that was on a gun rack. Finally, by stretching as far as she could, she got it.

The door handle jiggled again, and then the screen door closed. Gasping for air, she tried to regain a sense of calmness. It wasn't happening. She flew into the hall she had been before. She could see both doors.

Where were the men? Certainly someone was around. She grabbed her cellphone. Her hands shook so badly she could hardly push the speed dial. Stetson answered and before she could say much, he told her to stay put. He'd be right there.

She wished that hearing his voice made her feel better, but it didn't. Now the back door handle was turning. The lock was old, and she prayed it held. Damn, why had she hung curtains? She couldn't see anything out back.

Her fingers were cramping from the tight hold she had on the rifle. Tremor after tremor went through her. She could feel the sweat rolling down her brow.

She jumped at the sound of kicking. Oh God, where was everyone? The door moved. He was going to get in. Running was not an option. She had to protect Scotty at all costs.

The splintering of the door seemed deafening. Fear encompassed her, but she felt strange sense of purpose. Her hands stopped shaking and she held the rifle up and aimed it at the door.

All Storm noticed at first was the gun, aimed right at her. She heard a shot and she shot back. The intruder fell to the ground and Storm quickly grabbed their gun.

The shooter wore a black Stetson and a blue

bandanna tied around the face. On closer look, Storm recognized the intruder and her face felt as though all the blood had drained out of it. She felt woozy; she had a dead person on her floor.

Stetson raced through the front and Stamos through the back, both had guns drawn. Stetson took one look at her and he held her. He gently pried the rifle out of her hands. The whole thing seemed so surreal. She felt as though she was a bystander watching herself.

"There's no one else out there," Garrett said as he walked in the front. He stopped suddenly and his eyes widened. "Good Lord."

"Exactly." Stamos had grabbed a few towels and was putting pressure on the shoulder wound. "Call an ambulance and the police."

"Why? I don't understand why?" Storm could feel her face grow wet from tears.

"You know why. You tried to steal my man." Chrissy's smile looked demonic.

"You burnt down the barn, didn't you?" Stamos asked.

"Yep. Sam Evers told me to continue on in case he was taken away. I have a whole plan to execute and soon I'll be rid of the McCrory clan."

Feeling lightheaded, Storm swayed. She buried her face in Stetson's chest and cried.

"No really, what's the real story?" Garrett asked.

"I told you. Sam and me are one. He's going to marry me when he gets the money coming to him, but in order for him to have his big payday, certain people must die."

"Are you insane or what? You tried to kill my wife." Stetson helped Storm in a chair and charged over to where Chrissy lay. "What were you thinking? The Chrissy I knew was a sweet kid."

Chrissy gave him an eerie smile. "That's what I was thinking. You just see me as some wet nose, tagalong kid. Sam sees me as a woman. His woman. I could have been yours, but that bitch got in the way. So when Sam outlined the plan to kill her, I happily agreed."

"And the fire? What the hell was that all about?" Stetson's hands were clenched against his sides.

"He threw Sam under the bus. The rustling was all McCrory's doing. Sam never got his fair share. It was revenge and a distraction to get that broken down woman you call a wife alone."

The ambulance sirens were a godsend for Storm. She wanted Chrissy as far away from the ranch as possible. The smell of blood was making her nauseous and she felt bone tired.

Scotty woke up and Garrett graciously took him and Buck to his ranch. She knew she would always remember his kindness.

Stamos walked to her and kissed her cheek before he left. It was so sweet that she started to sob. Maybe she was sobbing about that or Chrissy or a billon other things.

Stetson picked her up in his strong arms as her body jerked with each cry. He carried her into the living room and sat her on his lap. He cradled her to his body and rocked back and forth.

Finally she quieted. It was over. She didn't even care if her father had been part of the rustling or not. She was safe in her husband's brawny arms, and that was all that mattered. She felt safe in trusting him, safe in loving him.

CHAPTER TWENTY-ONE

Epilogue

Storm loved days like this. Days where it was still cool but not chilly and everything was turning green, looking shiny and new. The sun was rising all orange and pink with a hint of purple.

She had just fed little Seth, bundled him up, and sat on the porch swing with him. It seemed to be his favorite. *What a beautiful child.* He had blue eyes with the longest lashes and his hair was coming in blond. He was born bald, which made for many unwanted jokes. He looked a bit more like her than Stetson.

Across the yard she could see Nellie sitting on her front porch with little J.J., Joseph Junior. Now that was a baby with big lungs. Sometimes Nellie would be beside herself when she couldn't get him to stop crying. It seemed Joe had some magic touch. J.J. quieted down every time Joe held him.

Storm had tried to explain a colicky baby to Nellie, but she often thought it was her fault. Storm couldn't wait for little J.J. to outgrow this stage.

Looking down on her precious son, she smiled as he cooed at her. The screen door opened and Buck bounded down the stairs and into the trees.

Scotty, the proud big brother and big cousin, came out in his pajamas and bare feet. He looked at Seth and frowned. "Are you going to spend the day with him again?"

"And with you too."

"Naw, I'm going to work with Daddy. He doesn't cry. Just make that Seft doesn't play with Buck. Buck doesn't like Seft."

Storm nodded and shooed him inside to get dressed. Next fall he'd be starting school. She had to admit she and Scotty had been through some hard times, but since Stetson came back, they'd been happy.

The screen door opened again. The heavy boots against the wooden floor gave him away. Stetson just stood there and stared at her.

"What? Do I have something on my face?"

Stetson shook his head and sat down next to her and Seth. "You, my dear, are glowing. Anything you want to tell me?"

Storm handed Seth to him. She loved watching them together. Stetson's hands were so big and Seth was so tiny. Stetson was a very hands-on dad and it made her proud. "No, I'm not pregnant. I'm just happy. I feel so very blessed to have you and the boys."

"All things considered, everything turned out for the best."

Neither said it, but she knew that they were both thinking about the recent trials. Sam Evens and Blue Sawyer got life without parole. They were lucky they didn't get the electric chair, but it seemed they both had important information. There were a couple other bodies found. Cowboys that had worked on her father's ranch and were thought to have left.

Chrissy was proclaimed incompetent to stand trial.

She was currently in a state hospital.

As it turned out, Storm's father didn't know about the rustling. Sam Evers manufactured proof to keep her father under his thumb.

Storm laid her head on Stetson's shoulder. How she loved this man. It had scared her at one point, but now it only made her stronger.

Her father had tried to mend fences and Stetson told her it was her call. She couldn't do it. Forgive and forget. She could maybe forgive, but she would never forget the horror he put her through. The worst was when he knew Stetson was the father and still called her a tramp. No, she couldn't have a relationship with him.

She had her own family now. One she was very proud of. One that loved one another. They worked hard during the day, but the nights with Stetson were sweet, sweet heaven.

Turning her head, she studied her handsome husband. He would never leave, she was certain.

"What? Do I have something on my face?" He gave her a slow sexy smile.

"Yes. A smile. I love you so much."

"What's not to love? I love you too, honey."

ABOUT THE AUTHOR

Sexy Cowboys and the Women Who Love Them...
Finalist in the 2012 and 2015 RONE Awards.
Top Pick, Five Star Series from the Romance Review.
Kathleen Ball writes contemporary and historical western
romance with great emotion and
memorable characters. Her books are award winners and
have appeared on best sellers lists
including:
Amazon's Best Sellers List, All Romance Ebooks,
Bookstrand, Desert Breeze Publishing and
Secret Cravings Publishing Best Sellers list. She is the
recipient of eight Editor's Choice
Awards, and The Readers' Choice Award for Ryelee's
Cowboy.
Winner of the Lear diamond award Best Historical Novel-
Cinders' Bride
There's something about a cowboy.

Other Books by Kathleen

<u>Lasso Spring's Series</u>
Callie's Heart
Lone Star Joy
Stetson's Storm

<u>Dawson Ranch Series</u>
Texas Haven
Ryelee's Cowboy

<u>Cowboy Season Series</u>
Summer's Desire
Autumn's Hope
Winter's Embrace
Spring's Delight

<u>Mail Order Brides of Texas</u>
Cinders' Bride
Keegan's Bride
Shane's Bride
Tramp's Bride
Poor Boy's Christmas

The Greatest Gift
Love So Deep
Luke's Fate
Whispered Love
Love Before Midnight

47949837R00137

Made in the USA
Middletown, DE
06 September 2017